ORUGL

THE

ATROCITY

OF

ERWANBA

JOHN W KURI

PUA NEW GUINEA

Paperback ISBN: ISBN: 978-0-6459322-1-8

First Published in 2023 by

First Nations Writers Festival International Limited

T/as First Nations Publishers

A Registered Charity (ABN 79 655 932 979)

2/53 Junction St, Nowra NSW 2540, Australia

Phone: +61 491 851 353

Email: firstnationswritersfestival@gmail.com

Web: www.firstnationswritersfestival.org

FB: www.facebook.com/firstnationswritersfestival.com

Line Edited: Anna Borzi AM 2023

Cover Design: Tim Axton

Typeset: Busybird Publishing

Printed and bound in Australia by IngramSpark

Dedicated to my mother; Julie Kopai MaieAmbo Kuri

"Singna mina diwo

Drana mina diwo

Spinde Gainde

Dire baire

Dingradiwo

Saaaa"

An old Gandia chant

The characters, names, location and events are fictitious. Any resemblance to real life situations is unintended.

All terms in vernacular are in the Kuman language.

Contents

Prequel:

Porugl Son of the Underworld

Porugl is born in a time when all life is ruled by the tribe. He is the grandson of Kande Kumugl chief of the Akenku Tribe in Gandia. Things change drastically for the worse when the chief dies without announcing who takes over. The chieftaincy of the Akenku Tribe is on the ropes and there is an intense struggle between the sons of Kande Kumugl for the leadership. Blood is spilt and family ties are broken.

Past sins and misgivings come into the light as tempers flare and loyalties begin to switch. The tribe is fractured between Porugl's father Gamba and his uncle Dingan who is his father's half-brother.

Porugl is caught in the crossfire and hurled into a legendary pit before he witnesses his sixteenth season. What happens after his descent into the pit is quite unexpected. He has heard tales about the pit in bed time stories told by his mother which does not even come close to what he sees in the realm of the Underworld. This is a place where magic, mystery and myth come together. It is a strange place where cave walls light up the caverns with brilliant luminance and inhabited by fantastic beings. Its sparkling crystal clear lakes and streams teem with all sort of creatures. He quickly finds out that he is not the first to be thrown down the pit. Three men have survived the fall previously and keep Porugl company. He becomes an avid swimmer and discovers amongst other things the many lakes in the realm. His time there brings him across two creatures; Nondo and Goglko.

The Underworld has its own rules and traditions. To live in the Underworld, he has to marry a spirit wife which he does. However, he still desires returning to Gandia. He has been told that there are some secrets in the Underworld he should never know; the greatest secret being Kerwanba, the ancient serpent who is Queen of the Underworld. The Underworld has been living in fear of Kerwanba since time immemorial. She rules with her strength and deadly fangs. It is said that she was the first in the Underworld. She fears that humans are growing in number in her domain and might begin trying to satisfy their curiosity. So she decides to cull the human population starting with Porugl's half breed. It is then that Porugl sees an opportunity to return to his homeland. He manages to escape her jaws and returns to Gandia, only to find that his father has been murdered by his half uncle and who has also made his mother pregnant. In a rage, he kills his father's murderer right after his mother gives birth to a still born baby. He has finally returned to Gandia but the Kerwanba rages deep in the bowls of the earth unable to get his name out of her head. The Underworld is in turmoil because word has spread out quickly to all the other realms that Porugl beat Kerwanba.

I

Bindekai

Porugl moved the firewood into the ash to keep the embers alive when he heard a voice. He felt around for his axe. All his sleepiness disappeared. A mountain breeze moved quietly, seeping through the forest. He had spent three nights near the ancestral burial site at the foot of the Bindekai peak, under an overhanging rock. Seeking answers.

Dew drops from a small tree all fell together suddenly and he froze. Keeping his gaze outward, he reached for his axe. He checked the other side. Still no sign. He peered over the flames and saw the axe wedged in one of the logs he had split during the day. Angered by his absent-mindedness, he reached for the axe, when something slipped and landed with a thud. He heard branches and overgrowth being pushed aside. The dark patches of the forest had eyes overwhelming him. His hands and legs trembled.

"Who is out there?" he said.

The flame went out, leaving the embers to give him little light.

"I'm warning you, I will kill you even if you are from the Akenku tribe. Now show yourself," he said with more energy to boost his own self-confidence.

Total silence enveloped the area. He crept over and got his axe.

"Kill him," shouted a voice from the darkness.

Suddenly, the forest erupted into a flurry of running feet and bodies scrubbing against the bushes and shrubs. Figures charged towards him from the dark with their axes out. Porugl swung his axe wildly and sprung into the forest. He knew this part of the terrain well and hid behind a thick tree. He saw three men with their faces painted black standing around the fireplace. One of them crouched and held his cheeks. The other two kept standing and scanned the area.

"He went that way," said the tall and muscular assailant, pointing in Porugl's direction.

"Let's return. We had our chance but missed it," said the other.

"Return? Look what he did to my face, I'm not returning until I kill that bastard," said the one who crouched near the fire place checking his face for blood.

"I think he is still here watching us," said the first. "Spread out."

The assailants put more wood into the fireplace and the smoke increased. They paced cautiously at arm's length from each other.

Porugl peeked around the tree quickly and saw them.

His hands, legs, and lips shivered against his will. Dew dropped continuously from the leaves of the tree and made its way down his spine. The damp earth and cold air made it hard to keep steady. The place lightened up, and the mist moved in. He bit his lip as the men approached the tree at the edge of the cliff.

The muscular warrior saw the path leading down to the village and studied it.

"He is here. He never left, no tracks," he said.

He motioned to the cut warrior to check around the tree. Porugl got ready. The big and slippery roots protruded from the trunk, making it difficult for the man to advance. He stepped carefully over the huge roots. Porugl moved at him swiftly with his axe the moment he glanced down to see where he stepped. The two other warriors heard a thud as the body hit the earth some distance below. They waited, not knowing who fell down the cliff. They called his name several times, then the muscular one beckoned the other to go and check.

"This is not going well," Kerwanba said to her minions. "I don't want to deal with more dead bodies, do something about it," she ordered.

They watched from a distance. Kerwanba couldn't intervene yet. She considered herself a superior being and didn't bring herself down to deal with humans. She had her minions to do that for her.

"Jump over the cliff," came a voice into Porugl's head.

"Huh?" he grunted, looking around to see where the voice came from and alerting the two attackers of his location.

"Good work Kimin-ege," said Kerwanba. "One more time."

"Your path is blocked," said Kimin-ege into Porugl's ear.

Porugl saw the cliff and a sense of déjà vu gripped him, remembering the time he jumped into the Sikewake cliff missing Kerwanba's jaws. At that time, he jumped because he knew he would land in water. But here, he didn't know what lay below.

The two warriors made their way around, and he had to make a decision. He had never been to the bottom of the cliff. He caught movement in his peripheral vision and swerved just in time to avoid a swinging axe. Before the second attacker swung his axe, Porugl leapt and grabbed his arm, holding the axe. The other man joined in and the three scuffled near the edge of the cliff until one of them tripped over a root and all three fell over. They clung to each other, falling down the cliff. Bones and skulls shattered when the three bodies met the ground with force. Porugl opened his eyes after a few moments. With blurry vision, he stared into the lifeless eyes of one attacker. Blood spilled out of his mouth. The other attacker lay beside them face down with his head smashed.

Kerwanba shook her whole body and cried, "Why do I have to do these things myself?"

Trees and bushes got pummeled as she slithered towards Porugl. Her ragged body ripped branches off and flung leaves into the air. She displaced rocks and boulders and paid no attention to anything else in front.

Porugl got up groggily and heard the commotion in the forest. He didn't know how to get to the path, but he had to go down. Without waiting to see the cause of the rumbling, he sprinted into the bushes. He jumped over rocks, ducked under branches, tripped over, got up and kept running downhill. The earth shook as a dislodged rock caused a huge landslide, sending rubble and earth further down. He skied down a slippery portion on his ass and in one motion got up and continued. There came into his view a house with smoke coming out of its thatched roof. He had to get there quickly.

No other creature or force could have created such a disturbance. It had to be her. But how could that be? She was in the Underworld, he thought. He walked up the small ascent towards the house and got his bearings right and his breath back. He came to the village after passing a couple more houses. The clamor had stopped behind him.

She watched Porugl reaching the main path leading into the village. Rage filled her eyes and became red. The minions shivered and struggled to keep out of her view. If she was going to punish anyone for this failure, they would be the first to feel her ghastly fangs.

"Get to work on the other two," she told the minions. "Now!"

The minions scurried away. The men were still sleeping when they arrived. Kimin-ege stung one and Gurr-toki stung the other. Both men woke with a fright. The three minions were in their natural, ghastly form. The men saw them and shook terribly. Kimin-ege explained that Porugl had escaped, and they had to track him and kill him right now.

"We are watching over your family for you, while you hide here, sooner or later, you will deal with Porugl, we are offering you the chance now to do that, if you succeed one of you could become chief, you are Kande Kumugl's sons," said Kimin-ege.

The two men thought about what to say next.

Agandua shouted at them, "Wake up from your slumber and track and kill him right now or we will hurt your wives and children."

They got their weapons and rushed out and the minions followed them.

Porugl didn't follow the main road to his mother's house and took a shortcut. The minions had already gone ahead and found him walking through the bushes. They told the two men who waited for him at a point he would approach.

Porugl walked through familiar territory, a place he frequented during his childhood. But this morning it felt strange. He didn't feel right and checked the fringes of the bush. The three assailants he killed made him cautious. Just then, an arrow shot past his neck, and he fell backwards. Someone was running to him and the footsteps were getting louder. He got up and took cover by some overgrowth. No one came from the front. Turning around, he saw a man charging at him with his axe out. The assailant would shoot him if he stood up, so he scrambled to the side. The man in front with the bow had his arrow loaded and waited for Porugl to show his head. Then he heard crashing in another part of the bush. He came out from his hiding place and the two men pursued Porugl. They saw Porugl come onto the main path.

Porugl joined a group of men carrying what looked to be a dead body. They had covered the body in leaves. The two men rushed through the bushes to see Porugl walking with the group of men. There was nothing they could do, and they stopped. Porugl continued until he was near his house and then left. He turned around and saw no sign of the two men.

He had been away from the village three nights at the foot of Bindekai. He needed to rest and have a proper meal. His journey had been tough and interesting. He figured Kerwanba was using all her powers to destroy him. He wondered if the beings in the Underworld knew about Kerwanba's recent attempt to kill him. They had told him that Kerwanba never interfered with humans in the Outerworld. Kewand Kumugl had told him that if she became involved, she would break the balance. He always wondered what they meant by 'balance', a term frequently used by creatures of the Underworld like Goglko and Nondo. Even Kewand Kumugl always referred to it.

Kerwanba came out of her abode, which meant that she was ready to do anything to end his life, even if it meant breaking the balance, he thought. The gravity of the situation became apparent to him as he came onto the track leading to his mother's house. Kerwanba had her powers at her disposal to carry out her plans, and he had none except his axe. He had to get word to Nondo or Goglko about what Kerwanba did. The more information he had, the better he would be prepared. Kerwanba maintained her authority in the Underworld with ruthlessness. Any creature who presented a challenge to her authority suffered pain at her fangs. She had the habit of not killing them but biting them and injecting her venom. Porugl had done more than challenge her authority. He had beaten her and this would set the pace for her revenge; he was sure.

2

Insomnia

Kerwanba tossed and turned in her lair. No one in her ancient memory had done what he did. She closed her eyes to sleep, but sleep had vanished. The tremors kept coming and the air and cave walls all repeated one word. She shut her mind and her ears, but it didn't stop. The word consumed her from within and if she didn't do anything about it, she would go insane. The scent of the freshly cooked pork and joyous laughter in Gandia all cradled his name. Happy feet danced and drums belted out victorious tunes into the atmosphere in his honor. The excited chorus of voices echoed across the valley for three days straight and broke the doldrums that had captivated the village for some time.

Everything happening above rekindled Kerwanba's thoughts of when she roamed these lands a long time ago. She didn't want to think about it.

"Minions," she screamed.

The minions assembled in front of her, shaking and ready to receive their instructions. Her voice rebounded off the cave walls and into the other realms. Creatures scrambled into their abodes upon hearing her screech. They knew the minions set out to do her evil bidding.

All the stories saturated the villages in the land and it did not get lost along the way. The leaves of the plants, rocks of the land, and marshes all resonated his name. The peaks and ravines echoed Porugl, Son of the Underworld until it reached the depths of the deep dark world where he had come from. The name bounced on the rock walls and caves leaping from crevice to crevice into the deepest parts of the unknown, to a place where no being had ever been, and right into the abode of an ancient creature, older than the Underworld itself. Kerwanba felt bruised and battered. Most of all, her pride shattered. The Queen of the Underworld coiled herself in pain. No creature existed without her knowing and no one dared to get in her way or disobey her. Kerwanba had been living in turmoil in the Underworld after that momentous day when Porugl triumphed over her at the cliffs of Sikewake. She thought of nothing else except the day when she would end his life. Whenever someone mentioned Sikewake, they thought of Porugl beating the age old serpent Kerwanba.

Kerwanba didn't attack him in the Outerworld. Attacking him would break the balance. She nearly broke it, driven by anger and rage. Kerwanba kept her deep, dark secret of the balance to herself. She knew some in the Underworld also knew about it, but didn't speak of it. Attacking him meant exposing her and the secret she harbored. She had her minions to do that for her. Her ancient memory taught her to be patient. She would wait to strike when he least expected it. But the stories circulating among the different realms hinted that Porugl slaughtered her at the sharp cliffs of Sikewake. Her wounds had healed, but the injury to her pride would never heal.

No one saw him scamper like a little girl, she thought. This time, the entire land will witness, when I pick limb by limb, muscle by muscle, tendon by tendon, until his bones are bare. I will break tradition if I have to. I will break the balance if that's what it takes.

"Underling," she hissed

Creatures in her domain quivered when they heard her and turned into their abode for fear of being in the way of her wrath. She tried to sleep, but something had disturbed her. The underlings' name kept ringing all around her and disturbed her sleep. Then a thought occurred. A slow and painful death until his last breath for his insolence sounded right. She hissed and slithered slowly out of her domain, determined to hurt him, starting with everyone he knew or loved in the Underworld.

"Dikamb," hissed the immense snake while making its way across the water.

The snake's curving body across the lake sent ripples of anger outwards. The cavern looked dark, dismal, and empty with her entry. All the light and life disappeared.

Kewand Kumugl heard the snakes breathing. His heart beat faster and louder than it had ever done before. Many in the Underworld expected the ancient serpent to unleash her fury upon him after his wife broke tradition. As the snake moved along the cave floor, all beings cowered in their abodes waiting to hear his deathly screams. He knew the time had come for her to make an example of him. Every night, he awaited his fate. He had ghastly dreams of the serpent ripping his head off.

"Dikamb," she hissed again.

The snake's voice stung the air, sending unseen shivers into every spine who heard her. There was total silence. She looked around and said, "I know where you are, Dikamb, come out."

Slowly, a figure appeared out of the lake.

Without looking up, Dikamb said, "Great serpent of the dark, why do you call me?"

Kerwanba looked at her and said, "Now I know why the underling left you. You are ugly."

"You killed our—"

Kerwanba grabbed Dikamb in her jaws and sunk her fangs deep into Dikamb's body, squeezing the life out of her. The echoes of her terrifying scream ricocheted off the cavern walls to all the realms of the Underworld. Kerwanba opened her mouth and gulped Dikamb. Drops of blood dripped down the snake's fangs as she turned her head to Kewand Kumugl's abode.

He sweated heavily and his heart thumped against his chest. He heard every slither as the snake made its way toward him. He fell with his face to the floor as soon as the serpent appeared.

Shaking and crying he said, "Oh ancient one of the deep dark, do not slay me. I have halflings to care for."

The snake's forked tongue considered him for a while as it moved in and out. Drops of blood splattered on the cave floor near his sweaty face, and he jolted.

"Your halflings are of no concern," she said and moved around his abode, which was not big enough for her to fit in. "You have a task to do. Fail me and you and all your halflings, including the ugly *gigl ambu* wife who has been expelled, will die. I will not allow a *makan nem* to intervene for you, succeed and you can get your wife back into the Underworld."

"Anything, tell me and I will do it," he said.

Being human, Kewand Kumugl didn't have the powers to traverse between the Underworld and the Outerworld to forage for food. Every time he asked other *gigl's* to share their food, and it became increasingly embarrassing for him. The Underworld beings looked with pity on him, but sometimes they shunned him. Others sympathized with him in this state and supported him.

Whilst making its way back, the serpent warned all creatures of the Underworld not to come into contact with Porugl or they would share the same fate as Dikamb. The creatures saw her red eyes and her ghastly fangs as she called his name. She crawled back to her abode. She re-established her rule and authority. Her minions would do what she wanted in the Outerworld.

3

At First Sight

The village buzzed with excitement. Porugl's return from the Underworld triggered stories that spread like the wind far and wide across the land. Those who told his story did it several times to listeners and made it even tastier each time by adding their own flavor to it. Young boys imagined themselves to be Porugl.

Old men recounted the stories of the great Kande Kumugl, and said, "It's all in the blood. He can and will do it. That's why he did it. No one else could have done it."

Every time a slightly unique version developed and distinct elements emerged, created by those who derived satisfaction from telling it. Young girls from neighboring tribes made it their business to get all the information they could about Porugl. They stood around in groups talking about him and giggled. In their mind, they would marry and have children with him. It didn't matter what the other girls said. All of them wanted to marry him.

"I don't care which world, this world or the Underworld, I was born to be his wife," said one girl.

"Is that so?" said another, and the conversation turned into a challenge to see which girl would become his wife.

"Oh stop it, the lot of you," said an old woman who passed by. "Porugl is married to a *gigl ambu*. How can you beat that?" This brought hysteria to the girls' conversation, and they plunged deeper into justifying why Porugl should marry them.

To the tribal enemy, Porugl epitomized the great and fearsome warrior Kande Kumugl, Chief of the Akenku. The storytellers cited to enemy tribes and said, "Kande Kumugl killed your father and your father's father. Porugl will do the same to you, it's in his blood."

The story changed dramatically and by the time it reached the outskirts of the surrounding enemy tribes, Porugl had slaughtered the terrifying mythical Kerwanba. The storytellers delighted in this, proudly proclaiming to the surrounding tribes, "He ended the ancient serpent. You are no match to him. He will destroy all of you."

This brought great distaste and uneasiness to the other tribes. Kande Kumugl's death brought an inward ease to the leaders of the other tribes. One man's dominance across the land had ended. When Porugl's tale rolled across the land, the rosy comfort the leaders enjoyed disappeared. The story broke out everywhere.

His tribesmen welcomed the stories like a refreshing shower of rain cooling off tensions and bringing confidence back into the tribe after a period of anxiety and apprehension during Dingan's rein. The other tribes treated the story like a disease, infecting fear and awe into the hearts of men. His absence in the village after beheading Dingan further added fuel to the rumours of his special powers from the Underworld. The village talked for days and the surrounding enemy tribes who slept better during Porugl's absence, now didn't sleep at all.

The elders became edgy. He was the only one remaining, a direct descendent in the bloodline of Kande Kumugl, to take over as chief. If he died or decided to relinquish his genealogy then, they would have to search for a new chief. They sat in the *yal yungu* discussing at great length while the village celebrated Porugl's return. Most of them didn't want to think that he would refuse the chieftaincy. The village was desperate and his return came at the right time. There was talk that the Kumoku, seeing them without a chief, had been planning to attack Akenku. They knew that a tribe without a chief was weak. A chief, once instituted, would assume all powers regarding tribal life within its own confines and to the surrounding tribes.

When Porugl ended Dingan's life, the Akenku had no chief. In a battle scenario, that would prove highly advantageous to the Kumoku and they knew it. Rumours came back to Gandia about the Kumoku's imminent attack.

"Can he handle it?" said an elder.

"We don't have time. Are you going to be responsible for battle strategy and giving out orders?" said another elder.

"He is already a man, he married a *gigl ambu* in the Underworld, and he killed Dingan, he is not innocent, he has made a man of himself already, we have to inform his mother and begin the process of instituting him, Gandia must know," said Ormar.

"He has not been initiated yet," said the first elder.

"Yes, the initiation is about to happen and he can take part, but we have to inform the people that our chief has returned," said Ormar. "They need to be confident again."

"And what of this rumour that the Kumoku want war?" asked another elder.

"It's not a rumour, they will strike anytime, and the most likely time is before we initiate Porugl, so we have to move fast here," said Ormar.

The elders recalled that the Akenku had never come across such a situation. For many generations, the Akenku enjoyed being the most powerful and celebrated tribe in Kondaland. Akenku warriors were the bravest and fiercest. They had the best lands, the biggest gardens and a colorful history to go with it. Every tribe looked up to Akenku with envy. It was an honor to be born into Akenku, was a statement they said. Girls from other tribes always wanted to marry into Akenku as a first choice.

That glorious history was now fading, and the elders were desperate to restore their name. They agreed that the situation didn't allow delay, and an announcement needed to be made as soon as possible. They would have to inform the mother. She was now the head of the family, with no other male relative alive.

They met Kondai, the mother, as she returned to her house, still weak from the birth of the still-born child.

"I think he went up to Bindekai, go check for yourselves," said Kondai and continued walking.

"Kondai, Gamba is gone, Yal Wai is gone and soon many of us will be gone to be with our ancestors. We failed you by not supporting you during these difficult times and we are sorry," said one of the elders walking faster towards Kondai.

"Stop it," she said, glaring at the elder who spoke.

All the elders stood transfixed.

"You deal with him. Why are you asking for my help?" she said without looking at them.

"He is the rightful heir to Kande Kumugl's leadership, but some things have to be sorted out first," said another elder.

"What?" she said, turning around. "He is still a boy. Give him some time."

"There is no time," the first elder said hastily.

She shook her head and flung her hands at the elders. "And what could be so urgent to make a man out of my boy so quickly?"

These elders have the nerve to come and demand Porugl be their leader, she thought. It was because of this tribe and the family legacy which resulted in the murder of my husband. What right did these old men have to come and demand?

"The Kumoku are preparing to go to war with us. They don't want us to build our confidence," said another elder.

She laughed and said, "They are a small and petty tribe.

I am humored to see you old men nervous about what an insignificant people say to a tribe as great as ours. If Kande Kumugl heard what you are saying, one of you would be at the receiving end of his axe."

This brought the elders to a halt. She had insulted them to their face. Without showing their distaste to what Kondai had said, they agreed with her but also mentioned Kande Kumugl was not around and this changed tribal dynamics.

"My family has all died for the cause of this tribe, and now you are asking me to give my blessing for my one and only son to lead you in war? I won't have it. Go and find your own leader. Let my son be an ordinary man. I have lost enough in my life and I will not lose my son again," she said.

"Lose what, mother?" said a voice behind them.

Porugl came out of the bushes and startled them.

Kondai broke out and wailed "*Aiyah na wana ume, na wana ume*," which means 'hail, my son is here, my son is here'.

The old men greeted Porugl with hugs and tears. They embraced him heartily, looked into his eyes and thought how closely he resembled his grandfather, and embraced him again. The thought made them weep even more. After emotions settled, the elders wanted to talk to him, but one look from Kondai was enough to stop them. The elders muttered to themselves about bringing up the matter another time. They bade Kondai and her son well and went on their way.

"Where did you get all these scratches and bruises?"

"It's nothing mother, what was that all about?" asked Porugl.

"Ah, forget it, just old men and their bickering. Forget them, they never visited me, I do have something to tell you though," she said with a smile as they walked back to her house.

"Why are you smiling, mother?"

"No, I'll let you find out for yourself."

"Mother," he said and stopped walking. "Just tell me."

By then they had arrived at the house, which now stood at a different location from the first hut he knew back then. The hot afternoon sun made his lips dry. He spent the three nights at the foot of Bindekai out in the open, and the experience with the attackers exhausted him. He needed to rest before going to the *yal yungu* or men's house.

"Maie, bring some water for Porugl."

He glanced at his mother in surprise. Kondai gestured for him to look at the entrance of the hut. A beautiful young girl came out carrying a bamboo container. She must be at least sixteen seasons, he thought. She had short hair, thick lips, and wide eyes. They exchanged glances. She smiled a courteous smile, and he smiled back. Did he see her somewhere before?

"Your water," she said and gave the bamboo to him.

Her husky voice had a tinge of energy. He took the bamboo container and drank, nearly coughing.

"I'm tired and hungry, I'm going in to rest, I'll prepare our food when I wake up," said Kondai and took the two heaps of sweet potato, fresh vegetables, and bananas brought by Maie into the hut.

Porugl made a desperate utterance to gain his mother's attention, but she ignored him. He stood there, feeling out of sorts. It seemed a lifetime ago when he had enjoyed the company of a woman. The thought brought back memories of his life with Dikamb, the *gigl ambu*. But he had never been with a human woman and so didn't know what to say or where to begin. Maie sat in the shade. Porugl kept standing and the ensuing silence prolonged in the afternoon sun.

"Are you two still out there?" called Kondai.

"We are here," said Maie.

Her voice sounded sweet. He sat down some distance from her and stole another glance. She also got a quick peek at him, and they both started laughing. He didn't know why, but he laughed like he had never laughed before in his whole life. And when she laughed, she exposed a set of clean white teeth which shone in the afternoon light. He looked longingly at her and could feel his manhood rising.

"That's more like it," came Kondai's voice.

"I don't know what this woman is talking about," he said, shaking his head.

They talked for a long time. Neither of them felt like moving when insects chirped at the onset of evening.

"The food is ready, come and have it while it is hot," said Kondai.

They didn't want to leave. Kondai had to call a second time to get them into the house. The three chatted while eating their dinner of pork from the celebrations.

"Maie, it gets cold and I am old, so you will sleep beside me," Kondai said.

Porugl went out to relieve himself. When he returned, his mother shoved sweet potatoes into the warm hot ashes. They would be baked and hot in the morning. He didn't see Maie, and his mind raced.

His mother sensed the question hanging in the air and said, "We are tired and going to sleep now."

He watched his mother make her way to the end of the hut, where it served as sleeping quarters. Thatched walls separated the room into two portions. He didn't think of anything else. He went and lay in the other room and stared at the ceiling. Though he gazed upward, his mind was far away, thinking about this beautiful young woman sleeping just inches away from him with only the wall separating them. He heard his mother murmuring something to Maie. He turned toward the direction of the two women and peeked through the spaces in between the thatched wall. It was dark and he couldn't see a thing. After a while, he heard her soft breathing. He endured the long night.

But something more terrible kept him awake for most of the night. Kerwanba came to the Outerworld to kill him. In all his living in the Underworld, she never did that. She used her powers to control the three men that attacked him. They painted their faces black, but one of them looked like a half-brother to his father. His father, Gamba, was born of Kande Kumugl's first wife. The great chief married two more women and had five sons. These sons and Dingan had all collaborated and killed his father when he was still in the Underworld. And even before that, they came and grabbed him, tied him to a pole and threw him down into the endless pit. When these half-brothers of his father heard that he killed Dingan, they all fled to the neighboring villages.

Kerwanba must have used her powers on the three of them. Two still remained. They were the ones who attacked him. He didn't feel completely safe and had to do something about it. He couldn't tell his mother or anyone. His mother had been living in fear and turmoil for quite a while. With his return, she seemed at peace. He didn't want to add fear to her life again.

Early the next morning, Porugl left the house and went to the *yal yungu* to clear his mind. On the way there, he met a group of boys going over to help a tribesman build his new house. He gladly followed them. It felt good to be amongst his own people, cracking jokes and sharing tobacco. They put down two enormous trees, but it didn't feel like work because all of them had a good time. He enjoyed the bonding with his tribesmen, something he missed out on. They talked about anything and everything and when it came to women; the discussion intensified.

In between splitting the tree trunks for the wall frame, Bolan asked Porugl, "Have you been home or not? I heard you have a visitor."

Porugl looked around and said with a smile, "No, I haven't, because your house is keeping me busy here," and they all laughed and made fun of each other.

The men and boys continued, and after two days, they erected the frame of the house. Women folk, including Maie, brought in bundles of *indaun* or strong grass to be prepared for the thatched roof. Porugl saw Maie bringing in her bundle and spun his gaze away. She dropped her bundle and walked with Kondai back to their house.

Tribal life took some time to adjust to. He had to be in the *yal yungu* at all times. The elders detested young married men frolicking and enjoying a secret moment with their wives. With the onset of thick hair growing around his face and other parts, the elders in the *yal yungu* kept a watchful eye on him and other young men like him.

Bolan had been watching Porugl and realized the poor kid didn't have a father around to tell him the little secret tricks of tribal life. He decided he would talk to him in the afternoon. After fastening the last knot, he asked Porugl to remain.

"Young man, is everything alright?" Bolan asked.

"Yes, everything is fine," said Porugl, frowning.

"I mean with Maie."

Porugl paused in his tracks and gazed across the land.

"Maie is there with mother. What can I say?"

"I don't know if Kondai has told you, but at some point, you have to decide whether she will be your wife or not. If you want her to stay, we have to inform her relatives. But if you want her to go, she will go with parting gifts."

Porugl looked at Bolan, puzzled. It was different here. Hanging around your wife for too long brought frowns and became a topic of discussion. The old men in the *yal yungu* criticized such behavior.

"Don't think about your wife too much. She belongs to the tribe. Women are here to bear your children, to raise them. Your business is to protect them at all costs. There have been wars and compensation demands because of women. Men have died over women, so don't linger around your wife too long," the elders always reminded the men.

The elders derided young married men caught following their wives for too long or being absent from the *yal yungu*. The elders spared no words and said, "Such young men will be the first to be killed in tribal warfare."

Bolan saw Porugl's uneasiness and comforted him.

"A true warrior is tactful on the battlefield and also with his wife. How can you defeat the enemy if you cannot rule in your own house? Don't pay any attention to the elders. They are just doing their job of priming young men to be good, powerful warriors. In the village, there are codes of conduct. You have to be tactful about when to talk to your wife, how to go and spend time with her. You have to develop secret codes or signals understood by you and your wife only."

Porugl shifted his gaze to Bolan.

"How?"

"You can have more time with her, but you have to be smart."

Bolan went on to describe some of the tricks he used with his wife. He would tell the old men he was going to the garden up in the mountains, but in fact, he would spend the night at his hut with his wife and children. Early in the morning, he would make his way up to the gardens in the mountain and return with food in the afternoon to the *yal yungu*. The elders couldn't say anything as he had proof. At other times, if he was feeling a sudden urge, he would say he was going out to relieve himself and went home to his wife.

"Always return to the *yal yungu*," Bolan said. "In that way, you are also looking out for the tribe when you return."

The Akenku had many enemies. Over the course of generations, they had battled with most of the surrounding tribes. Unresolved disputes ended up on the battlefield. The Akenku didn't start most of these fights, but never backed down from any challenge by another tribe. This school of thought preceded Kande Kumugl. The scars from these wars remained, and the Akenku remained vigilant, knowing that enemy tribes could attack or stage an ambush anytime. Every child born into the Akenku heard about these battles from generations past. The elders told them where the battled took place, whose family it concerned and the outcome.

"One day, you and I will be the elder telling our young warriors exactly what they are telling us now. It's all about being skillful and responding to situations. It's good training for warriors to be tactful in battle. The fight can change direction at any point in time, and a warrior has to decide in an instant what to do."

Porugl felt better already.

"Porugl, everyone is doing it, that's why the tribe exists," he said and laughed. The two walked towards the *yal yungu* as the sun set across the land of Gandia.

4

The Initiation

Several days after talking to Bolan, Porugl left the *yal yungu* to visit his mother and Maie. To his dismay, his mother didn't give them any time to be alone. This made him restless all throughout the night. He had not developed any secret codes or signals and was determined to get this part of his life going.

He woke up fresh and early, eager to continue where he left off. "Mother, I am having one of the sweet potatoes," he said, pulling out one baked in the hearth.

He patted the sweet potato and blew off the ashes. The warm aroma of the sweet potato filled his nostrils as he stepped out of the hut into the cool morning air. The hot food in his hand felt good. This moment gave him a sense of nostalgia and brought back memories of the dreadful day when men caught him and tossed him into the endless pit. He didn't have the condition anymore. His life in the Underworld had healed him and taught him many things, but he rarely spoke of his life in the depths of the earth. It would attract more rumours and controversy, which he didn't want. What he wanted now was to start his life like a normal man.

"Where is Maie?" he asked when his mother came out.

"Maie cannot be with us for a couple of days."

"Why?"

His mother shook her head and looked at him.

"Why do you want to know women's private issues? Get out of here before I shame you in front of the *yal yungu*."

He ground his teeth and swung his axe with much energy at the plants nearby. The dew felt cold on his leg as he passed by. When he arrived at the *yal yungu*, one of the elders told him about the initiation. He had completely forgotten.

"All the warriors and initiates have gone already to the foot of Bindekai. You will do well to hurry and catch up with them. Have you got your axe?"

"Yes," said Porugl.

"Then be on your way now," said the old man.

The elders had talked about the initiation for some time now. Warriors told of how they stayed in the forest and hunted for many days without any food. The elders warned all the young men to be ready. They ceased all courting activities with girls from the neighboring villages. Visits to their mother's house didn't happen as often as they used to. Every night, the young men expected some form of an announcement from the elders. For many nights, the announcement didn't come, making them restless. In the meantime, the elders told the young men to continue improving their skills.

In the Underworld, Porugl had no need for a bow and arrow, so he didn't practice the skill to craft one. There was no need for fencing, houses, gardens, or axes. But he did master one skill, and that was tracking animals. In the Underworld, he enjoyed traversing the deep cavern lake. After a long period of eating berries brought by his *gigl ambu* wife from foraging in the Outerworld, he decided to add meat to his diet. The cavern lake was a world of its own, teeming with life. All manner of underwater creatures and beings lived in the cavern lake, and the deep crevices in the rocks below the water provided the perfect surroundings for these creatures to dwell and populate.

Porugl sprinted up the mountain track. He could not miss this important tribal event. Every Akenku warrior went through the initiation process. How would the seasoned warriors and other boys see him? He thought. It didn't look good one bit. His story of returning from the Underworld slowly faded. Missing the initiation would trigger another round of stories in the village again about him. He didn't need that sort of attention at the moment.

He saw the footprints of the troupe leaving early in the morning. The initiates gathered around a group of seasoned warriors.

"You will be out here until such a time when you see the next full moon, sleep where ever you can, under the trees, in the cave, beside the foot of Bindekai. Your *deemaima* or axe is your life," said one of the seasoned warriors.

The warriors went on to explain what had to be done. The young boys had to make themselves a full quiver of arrows and a bow. They would then break into hunting parties and hunt wild pigs, cassowaries, possums, birds, bats, and cuscuses. The young warriors couldn't return to the village empty-handed and they couldn't eat anything during the period.

The elders had the skill to determine whether it would be a dry season or wet season or when the next full moon would appear just by looking at where the sun rose and set. For generations, this skill determined the type of activity the tribe engaged in.

"You will eat no food during this time you spend here," said one of the seasoned warriors.

"We will know if you cheat, we will know if you eat," said another warrior, and looked around at all the young boys. "You will bring shame to you and your family and this will be your long-lasting legacy in the tribe."

"You all know who Kupme is," said the first warrior. All the boys nodded.

Kupme had failed his initiation many seasons ago by eating. We relegated him to be the village handyman, which was a better option than expulsion or death.

"If you don't want to join him, then do as you are told," said the warrior. The elders and my brothers have shown you all you need to know. Show us you are man enough to leave your mothers and enter the *yal yungu* as a warrior."

The young boys waited for the warriors to be out of sight before forming their own groups. Porugl stood there, not knowing what to do or say. For most of his young life he spent in the Underworld and got accustomed to the ways of life in the Underworld. While boys his age had been taught how to craft an axe or a bow and arrow or build a house. None of the boys invited him. They stood in their groups watching what he would do next with smirks on their faces. He sensed them watching him.

"Let's see how this boy from the Underworld can hold up here," said one.

"Don't help him," said another.

"He is more concerned about his wife," said yet another boy, and they all laughed.

With his arrival, most of the talk had been about him. Some of the boys who considered themselves to be popular around the village quickly succumbed to the shadows of Porugl's story and resented him. But none of the boys dared to challenge him publicly after he swiftly put an end to Dingan's life. Inwardly, they didn't like the attention he got from all across the land. Most of the young boys courted young girls from other villages. These girls asked too many questions about him and the boys hated answering their questions.

"Don't worry, Porugl, I'm with you," came a voice behind him.

He turned around to see Waine. He didn't believe Waine at first and thought he was making a joke, because Waine always made jokes. People liked him but didn't take him seriously. He had a smaller build than most of the boys and had a hooked nose.

Waine kept looking at him with earnest eyes and said, "Well, are you just going to stand there? The birds and animals won't give themselves to us easily."

"Alright, where do we begin?" said Porugl.

"The first thing is to find the palm that produces the strongest bow string," said Waine as he walked across the forest.

He then explained to Porugl the intrinsic basics about crafting a solid and everlasting bow.

"Those thick heads don't know how to craft a bow and bowstring that will serve a lifetime."

"A bow for a lifetime?"

"Yes brother," said Waine, smiling.

Porugl imagined what it took to make an everlasting bow, but he had his doubts. He kept walking behind Waine as they set off deeper into the forest.

"We are near," said Waine, and stopped to get his bearings right. "The palm we are after should be over the ridge. Let's hope the others haven't gone there before us."

After some time of treading into the forest overgrowth, they came to the place Waine had pointed out.

"Is this it?" asked Porugl.

"Ahh, this is it," said Waine, and he hugged the tall palm tree.

Porugl helped Waine climb the palm and cut the leaves down.

"The bowstring is made from the spine of the leaves," said Waine while cutting the leaves. "The trick is to find the right girth of the spine. It cannot be too thin or too thick."

He continued to lecture about the art of making an everlasting bowstring. He taught Porugl how to cut strips from the spine and the curing time needed for the strips to be submerged in water.

"If you do it right, you will never use another bowstring again, Porugl. I know you are a powerful man, so I want to craft one bowstring to match your strength, one bowstring which will never snap."

Waine then told Porugl to go and find a *waisime*, which was the strongest bamboo to make the bow. Porugl returned with a long *waisime* bamboo shoot and Waine informed him that two groups of boys had come for the palm leaves. Porugl cut the bamboo and used his axe to give shape to the bow under the watchful guidance of Waine.

"How do you know so much about this?" Porugl asked.

"My father taught me."

Waine told him that he took from his father and grandfather, both master craftsmen. His grandfather had crafted one for Kande Kumugl as a gift, and it lasted a lifetime. Kande Kumugl never used another bow and bowstring again in his vibrant warrior's life. While warriors held their bow with one or two extra bowstrings, in case the bowstring snapped, Kande Kumugl didn't. Many had tried to imitate the elite warrior without success.

"We have to evict all unwanted juices, then we let them cool down for a while before sinking both the bow and bowstring in water," said Waine.

They spent the afternoon smoothing out the rough edges. Porugl split the bamboo in half along the nodes and cleaned out the seam where the nodes met, making a long bamboo tube to lay the bow and bowstring in. They placed the items in the bamboo tube which had water in it.

"Now we wait while these two get acquainted with each other," said Waine. "It's complete for now and I'm hungry."

"I know," said Porugl, "but we have to look for some place to shelter tonight."

"Hahaa," Waine cut in. "You should have thought about that before you placed them in the bamboo tubes. Now you cannot move it. They are getting married, man and wife. If you disturb them, you will not end up with a powerful bow and bowstring."

"So what are you saying?" said Porugl.

"I'm saying we have to find shelter not too far away. We can't have animals or rain or anything to disturb these two during the night. It is their first night and the only night that will last forever."

"Waine!" said Porugl and looked at him, already incensed at his references.

"Hey, this is how you treat the bow and bowstring, the curing time is the most important time of all. For your bowstring to last forever, you have to set it out like this. You will know once you try," said Waine.

"Alright," said Porugl and mentioned he was going to make a shelter.

Darkness crept into the forest, and the night insects and animals made themselves known. Porugl and Waine had built a temporary shelter where they tried to make themselves conformable. Smoke came out from different parts of the forest, where groups of young men settled for their first night away from home. Back in the village, mothers and fathers saw the smoke and thought about their sons.

The next day started early and Porugl lit the fire. A hot baked sweet potato from his mother's fireplace would do really well now, he thought. Waine woke from his slumber.

"We have to take these two out," said Waine.

Waine had completed heating the bow and bowstring over the embers of a slow fire. He mentioned to Porugl that the items showed no signs of stress. The time was right to hook the bowstring onto the bow. They would know if Waine crafted an everlasting bow and bowstring. The sun rose, and both felt pangs of hunger.

"You go first," said Waine and handed Porugl his bow and bowstring.

The slow heat caused the bow to stretch on its inner side, giving its slightly curved shape. If the treatment failed, the bow or bowstring would snap.

"Now is the time, Porugl," said Waine.

Porugl braced himself to hook the bowstring onto his bow. He placed one end of the bowstring onto the bow and he bent the bow with his knees to hook the other end to the bowstring. Neither bow nor bowstring gave in. He tried harder, but the two didn't budge. He released his grip and breathed a little. He tried again and his hands and knee shook, but the bow and bowstring did not succumb and still held their ground. Beads of sweat formed on his forehead and his veins showed clearly. This was a challenge between what they created and the craftsman. He didn't want to let Waine see him give in and, with all his might, pulled the bow down again for the third time. The veins on his neck bulged incredibly and Waine grimaced, thinking, sooner or later, either his veins might pop, or the bow would snap. With a mighty pull, he slipped the end of the bowstring into its place and released his grip. The bowstring took the bow in with a sharp and tight twang.

"That's the agreement," smiled Waine, and told Porugl to test the bowstring.

He pulled on the bowstring, releasing a high resonating vibration when his fingers let go. Waine didn't have to say anything, as Porugl immediately fell in love with his first and everlasting bow. He momentarily forgot about Waine, who also had to do the fitting of his bow.

"What are you going to do for me, Porugl?" Waine announced proudly into the forest with both his hands wide open.

"I don't know what to say. How can I repay you?" said Porugl.

"Ah, the great Porugl, Son of the Underworld, doesn't know how to repay Winny Waine," said Waine, raising his voice.

The boys and girls back in the village called Waine, 'Winny Waine' whenever they teased each other. They thought it would make Waine feel hurt, but in fact, Waine felt good when they called him that. It was his trademark name, and he savored the attention that came with it. Whatever Waine lacked in his physique, he made up for with his sharp tongue.

"I am your brother forever," said Porugl.

This statement from Porugl stopped Waine, and he looked back at him.

"I like that, my brother forever," said Waine.

Waine placed his bowstring on the bow with Porugl's help. Both men tested each other's bows.

"Porugl, take it easy on mine," said Waine

Satisfied, they went to prepare their arrows. By the time the sun set, both boys had collected and shafted a lot of canes for the arrows. The two also cut a couple of branches from a special tree used for arrow heads. They used tree sap to gel the arrowhead into the canes. They made smooth arrows, jagged arrows and wide tipped arrows. Both of them worked well into the night and dozed in the temporary shelter, too tired to think about food.

In the following days, Porugl and Waine tracked animals and set traps. Accompanied by hunger and tiredness, both continued, occasionally coming across some of the other initiates. The days trailed along and Waine complained much about food. Porugl also felt hungry but didn't want to encourage Waine, so he didn't respond. They laid many traps in the forest, and after several days of returning empty-handed, they caught their first animal; a big lizard with a flap-like structure around its neck and a very long tail. They heard stories of how this lizard used its tail to whip other animals and even humans. They skinned it and dried the skin in the sun. Then they smoked the lizard and offered it to the spirits of the forest.

A similar creature called Teme lived in the Underworld. It kept to itself in its abode at the far edges of the cavern lake. He never saw Teme in the central part of the realm, where all the creatures and beings congregated. He occasionally bumped into Teme in the water. Teme would be swimming back to its abode with its catch in its jaws. After spotting its prey from above, the fierce hunter plunged into the water at speed, using its sharp claws and teeth to capture its prey. Porugl found this interesting and studied its hunting habits.

Porugl missed the taste of meat, after many moons in the Underworld, and had been considering a variety of fishlike creatures to boost his diet. Teme hunted many animals and the best indication came from the big lizard. One of the fishlike water creatures it hunted had similar features to the fish he used to see in the river back in Gandia.

From that time on, he tracked and hunted the fishlike creature as well. It tasted good and didn't cause any issue for Teme. He expanded his skill set to tracking and trapping bats. His encounter with the angry dwarves who had chased him with the *gwika* leaf in his hand had shown him many holes and smaller caves where bats lived. Occasionally, he went up the treacherous path to that same place and return with a big splash in the lake, with all the bats he had trapped. Underworld beings studied him and noted that while the three other humans depended on their *gigl ambu* wives to bring them food, Porugl foraged for himself by improving his skills as a natural hunter. They appreciated that he gained those skills in such a brief span of time and labelled Kewand Kumugl and the other two humans as lazy.

Waine and Porugl returned from another tracking run. Waine caught a bandicoot while Porugl returned with a waterfowl. Both slumped and rested in their shelter. After a while, Porugl got up and started plucking the feathers off the fowl. Occasionally, they heard the chatter of boys from the other groups somewhere in the dense forest.

"What are you doing?" asked Waine

"I'm going to prepare it."

"Can you prepare the bandicoot as well," said Waine and rested.

A sizzling sound woke Waine. A delicious aroma came from the direction of the sound and entered his nostrils. Porugl turned the spit around and juices from the roasted bird fell onto the embers and sputtered, releasing its mouth-watering whiff into the surroundings. Waine saw the golden brown fowl and turned away when Porugl noticed him. To hide the lump of saliva, he struggled to swallow. If he had it his way, he would grab the roasted bird and crunch it, bone and all. Why is he doing this? Does he not feel hungry? He thought. The bandicoot was grilled already and placed near the fireplace.

"Porugl, we have smoked a lot of bats and a cuscus, and now this. Let's have some to gain our strength. I'm sure all the others are doing it," he said, still looking away.

He didn't reply directly to Waine's suggestion and said they had enough smoked animals. Now they had to wait for the full moon. They could not go through smoking another animal again for fear of succumbing to hunger. Porugl had swallowed a lot of sticky saliva that afternoon.

"Here come and salt your bandicoot," he said to Waine, trying to lighten up the afternoon.

"You salt it," said Waine.

"I'm salting the bird and you need to salt the bandicoot."

The hunger and exhaustion took its toll on both of them. They had bonded well initially. But as the days dragged on, Porugl's insistence that they eat no food frustrated Waine. He resented Porugl and regretted he chose to team up with him.

"We have passed already, we caught animals, we went without food for many days now, what more test is there? We have crafted our bows and arrows. We need to eat or we will die of starvation," said Waine.

Despite feeling weak, Porugl felt hilarious and wanted to laugh.

Waine dramatised everything in his life and always avoided physical work. During discussions about building a new house or making a fence, he took part enthusiastically. He would cut in more often and add his piece of mind about where he thought the best tree to be used was located or where to look for the strongest bush vines. But when the time came to go into the forest and do the things they discussed, he always had an excuse not to go, like bumping his toes on a tree stump. He would limp and make a big show of it. Once he turned around the corner of the bush, he straightened up and returned to walking normally.

His other trick was remembering that he had an important task to do and leaving the work party. The habit got on the nerves of the villagers. While some put up with it, others called him names. Some elders berated him, while others didn't bother. People liked to hear him talk. With his funny-looking face, everything he said turned out to be funny. Even when he didn't mean it to be funny, they still laughed nonetheless. Everyone knew his attitude and also enjoyed his company. He was fun to be around.

Porugl had been expecting some kind of reaction from Waine when they went without food for days. When he mentioned that they would die of starvation, he struggled to contain his amusement. He smiled to himself, shaking his head, as Waine rambled on. But it did come to the point where he had enough of Waine's persistence. He thought of getting up and tearing all the smoked animals they had prepared into shreds and stuffing them down Waine's mouth. He too felt the hunger pains and needed to get his mind off food quickly or he would snap.

"Where is the salt?" asked Porugl.

Waine heard him but didn't answer.

Porugl searched around and found the pouch of salt stuck in one of the poles supporting the shelter. His father, Gamba told him salt was made in the lands to the South. He dipped his finger into the salt pouch and patted the roasted bird, keeping his mind on the salt to distract himself. His stomach grumbled loudly as the delicious scent entered his nose. The roasted bird looked inviting. It was quite a while ago, and he couldn't recall the exact details. But he did remember some of the main things. Amongst other things like kina shells, medicinal herbs and animals, salt was a coveted item of trade.

Salt came from a far corner of the lands towards the south near the shaman Yal Wai's original village. The salt makers baked the salt from a stream, which had a very strong stench about it. This stream flowed continuously out of the ground and no vegetation grew near the stream. No other place had such a stream flowing out of the ground. For generations, this village, known as the salt people, supplied salt to all the known lands. Traders from different villages and lands came and exchanged food, shells, and pigs for salt, or mundi. Many men didn't touch their food unless it had salt. It was such a treasured ingredient that many gatherings were put on hold if salt was not available.

He turned around to see Waine, still fast asleep and snoring. The urge to take a quick bite of the roasted bird rose exceedingly. He put the bird over the embers and studied Waine, who had his back to him. The evening arrived, and the fire glowed, emitting a soothing warmth. Porugl made himself comfortable opposite Waine. Around midnight, he heard some movement to see Waine sneaking to where they hung the dried and smoked meat. He reached for the roasted bird when Porugl caught sight of him and they tussled around in the shelter. Without their energy, they tumbled around, leaving them both weak and breathless. Waine nearly fainted and drifted back to sleep. During the night, he became delirious and spoke gibberish.

Porugl felt strange as he lay down, exhausted. Something hovered above, smothering him. He tried to call Waine, but no words came out. His hands and legs were numb. His body lifted and became suspended in mid–air. He had no strength to break free and struggled to look around. He didn't know whether he opened his eyes or whether it was a dream.

"You made a promise," came a voice from the forest. "You made a promise to avenge our son."

"Our son?" said Porugl.

"Yes, your son, our son," came the voice again.

Porugl saw a figure coming out of the darkness and reaching for him. He tried to get away, but the figure kept coming to him and bringing him into itself. He could not break free from the grasp the dark figure had on him and his breathing became more difficult to the point where he could not breathe anymore. In an instant, with all his might and energy, he yelled, flinging his arms into the air. Something was shining brightly above. What is this he thought and cleared his eyes. There above him, the full moon shone in all its glory. Waine had not flinched in all the clamor. He shook Waine.

"Look," he said, pointing to the moon.

Waine gazed at the moon and went back to sleep.

The boys rose early in the morning. The promise of food gave them the energy to gather their stuff and return. Along the way, they met other teams. Some of the seasoned warriors arrived on the way and kept an eye on them. They didn't talk. At the last bend before the village, mothers exploded into a chorus of wailing when they appeared. Porugl saw Kondai and Maie and walked faster with the little energy he had in his legs. The elders welcomed them back into the village. During the night, the young warriors had their ears and noses pierced. They still didn't have any food yet. All the while, these young warriors watched as the older warriors and elders dined on what they had brought in. The village prepared a big feast for them the next day to inaugurate the young boys as men.

5

Ambai Kango

While the initiates went about establishing themselves with the announcement of marriages, making of new houses and gardens, and paying of bride price, Porugl had one final task to complete. He wanted his wife and mother to be free of any threats, and Kerwanba still hung in his mind. He had to put an end to his fears and carry out his plan in the night. His quiver of arrows was full and the thought of seeing his bow in real action, after all the practice, excited him. Except for a couple of elders, the *yal yungu* was empty on that night. One elder made his way to his part of the *yal yungu* to sleep. The other sat near the fireplace and took out sweet potatoes already baked.

He took down his bow from the roof as the two elders watched. They gave him puzzled looks, and he smiled at them. The elder gave him a baked sweet potato, and he ate.

"Hunting?" said the elder at the fireplace.

Porugl thought about how to respond. People hunted in the night when the moon glowed. The moon had moved on already.

"I need more practice," he said.

"Your grandfather had one exactly like yours," said the elder and retreated to his corner.

Porugl spent some time before he stepped out. The two half-brothers to his father lived at the back of Dawake village toward the side of a ridge. His strange experience during his initiation made him aware that he had to eliminate everyone that posed a threat to his family. After the grand feast hosted for the initiates, he asked around and found out that the two men left their families in Gandia and went to Dawake after they heard he killed Dingan. Their mother was a Kumoku woman. He had killed three already. He would deal with the remaining two tonight. The dark night made it difficult, but he knew the path and crossed the river. He passed the Dawake village quietly. A dog barked, and he stood still. The dog ceased barking, and he carried on, but then the dog began barking again. He didn't stop and kept going.

"Who goes there?" said a man's voice.

Porugl ignored him. He didn't use a fire torch, as it would draw unnecessary attention. He arrived near the house and stepped into the bushes near the house. Light streamed out of the house and he heard coughing. They had not slept yet. He threw a small rock at the front of the house. He waited a while and threw another one again. He heard talking in the house and threw another one.

"Hey who is it?" said someone.

The two men came out. One held a fire torch, and the other held his bow, looking out into the night. The fire torch proved more advantageous for Porugl than it did for the two men. He saw clearly two of his father's half-brothers. They could not see him. He let loose one arrow at the man with the bow and quickly reloaded. The one holding the fire torch didn't grasp the imminent danger before rushing back inside. He felt something piercing his back and out of his stomach. He made no sound when he fell. The fire torch fell to the floor and caught on the walls. The house was burning.

Porugl stood for a while before walking out of the bushes to the burning house. He dragged the one outside into the house. The second man was still breathing, but it would be for a short time only. He crouched down to both of them and told them his name.

"I killed the other three, did you know that?" he asked.

He returned to his *yal yungu* in Gandia and went straight to sleep, content that he had killed everyone who took part in his father's murder.

The next day he left the *yal yungu* or men's house and went down to his mother and Maie. As he got closer to his mother's hut, he heard a commotion. He ran to the hut to find Maie in an argument with Dengg. Kondai stood between the two young women.

"You have come a long way for nothing," said Maie with her hands on her hips.

"Me?" you have been wasting your time here. Who is your father? Call his name?" said Dengg, squinting her eyes.

They both stopped when Porugl arrived.

"Let him decide for himself," said Dengg and glanced admiringly at Porugl.

Dengg hugged him. Not knowing what to do, he hugged her, while Maie shot a riveting look at both of them. Maie's gaze pierced him and he broke free from Dengg's embrace, who wanted to keep hugging him. Dengg, a slim and fair-skinned young woman, came from the Kumoku tribe. They respected her father in the Kumoku tribe.

"Dengg has also come to be with us for a while. Whatever you do, Porugl, remember what happened to your father," said Kondai.

Porugl didn't say anything. He felt closer to Maie as she was patient, kind, and full of laughter. He had not experienced Dengg yet.

"The two will remain here with me until such a time when you decide whom you will marry or when one of them decides to leave," said Kondai.

He had to sort out who would remain to be his wife. He saw no way out. The beauty of the two women made the task harder. He could marry both women at the same time, he thought. But it was not customary to do so, and it was never done. He was not going to create another round of stories in the land again.

As days passed, Maie and Dengg remained with Kondai. Each one tried to outdo the other in all manner of duties and behavior. The days dragged on and Porugl become more agitated and restless. He had already seen the white sticky fluid at the tip of his penis after dreaming one night. He quickly rushed out of the *yal yungu* to avoid being spotted by one of the warriors or an elder. This was too much for him. Just when he thought he was going to be with Maie, he was away from her again. How could he visit one when the other was still around in the same house? It boggled his mind with so many questions. Maybe I'll see both of them at the same time, he thought. This would be outrageous. What if I build a new hut for one? But building a hut for one would be a clear indication of his choice. He didn't want to hurt either of the two women.

Meanwhile, both women worked furiously at being chosen. The garden plots showed no weeds and house cleaning happened daily. Both women prepared food with immaculate care and treated the animals like babies. Kondai enjoyed every moment. They pampered her and frequently asked if she needed anything. She smiled to herself, wondering if the two could remain.

Porugl completed the manly tasks, maintaining the fences and garden drains. He also had a large banana and sugarcane plot to attend to. Banana bunches had to be covered with leaves woven tightly around the bunch, and sugarcane had to be bundled around a long pole. This promoted growth.

Both women worked beside him. He never got a chance to sweet talk one, as the other was always within earshot. All talk was business and no pleasure.

This is cruel, he thought. Two women in my house and I cannot see even one of them. While these thoughts dragged on within his mind, the work on Kande Kumugl's lands, which he inherited, seemed like a breeze, and the new gardens sprouted with healthy growth. He saw the sticky fluid the second time and was out of the *yal yungu* in a flash. Ormar noticed the uneasiness in him for some days. He heard about the two young girls and noticed Porugl's demeanor change lately. He decided it would be best to talk to Porugl's mother first.

It was also an opportunity for him to see Kondai. Ormar wanted to take Kondai in as his second wife or *kambe nongwa*. Everyone in the village agreed Kondai needed a man around the house, especially the elders. As with all other issues, the elders would repeat "What belongs to the tribe stays in the tribe," and that included, men, women, children, land, animals, and the whole works. While the prospect of marrying into Kande Kumugl's family seemed attractive, certain obligations had to be fulfilled first.

Kondai was chatting with the two girls in their hut when Ormar announced his arrival. The three women came out of the hut and greeted Ormar.

"A good morning to you all," said Ormar.

Kondai asked about his early morning visit. She knew Ormar had been trying to marry her. Some of the womenfolk also told her about his intentions. She did give it some thought, but right now, her mind and focus were on the two young women who wanted to marry her son. It felt awkward to her that she should expose her feelings or interest to the man who wanted to marry her in public.

"I hope it's important. We are leaving for our gardens."

Maie and Dengg found that to be amusing because they attended to the gardens and animals already.

"I'm sorry for disturbing you so early. We need to talk."

"Then we will leave you," said Dengg, smiling.

"You two stay right there," exclaimed Kondai.

"Ahh Kondai, I agree to them leaving, as this concerns the two young girls."

Kondai paused for a moment and said, "All right, don't go too far."

When the girls had left, Ormar explained his concern.

"We have to make a decision. The more we prolong, it will lead Porugl to do things we may regret. All the young warriors his age are married. That's how we contain our young warriors in upholding the tribe."

Ormar saw her thinking about what he said while he thought about how he would make her his wife. He would bring his choicest pig as a parting gift to the girl who would leave. The thought made him comfortable, and he saw a way to get her approval.

"I cannot tell the two girls. It has to be you or one of the elders," she said.

"We will be giving *komba bir* to the Daneku, the day after tomorrow. We will sort it out after that," said Ormar.

After talking at length, Ormar left her. He would brief the elders in the afternoon. Kondai was sullen all throughout the time leading to the announcement. Inwardly, she felt close to both Maie and Dengg. The two young women became more like daughters to her. She had one daughter, but she married into another tribe and lived her life. If she had her way, she would tell them both to stay and Porugl could build another house. Maie and Dengg also felt uneasy at seeing her unsettling persona. But for now, they had to fulfill their tribal obligations in the *komba birr*. She would remind Porugl to go and harvest all the *komba* or red pandanus along the riverside and prepare it for the Daneku tribe.

Some seasons ago, when Porugl still lived in the Underworld, the Daneku, a tribe up north had performed an *amugl birr* to the Akenku. The Akenku tribe had traveled to the Daneku village and brought back heaps and heaps of *amugl* or pandanus. The *komba* or red pandanus season arrived in Gandia, signaling Akenku's turn to perform a *komba birr* to the Daneku. While *komba* grew in low altitudes, *amugl* only grew in high altitudes. Gandia and all the villages in Kondaland savored both foods. As such, villages in the low altitudes gave red pandanus during its season, to a village of their choice in the higher altitudes. The receiving village would then return the favor with *amugl* or pandanus when it was the pandanus season. The exchange of food allowed young men and women from different tribes to meet each other. It also provided a time to meet and forge new friendships or strengthen existing ones.

Porugl heard his mother's voice and stepped out of the

yal yungu. His mother didn't come at all to the *yal yungu* unless it was to give him food or tell him about something important. She must have some news about Maie and Dengg, he thought.

"Go to Kamawagle and harvest all your *komba*."

Porugl didn't say anything. He heard the elders discuss the event in the *yal yungu* but right now; it was not one of his priorities. He had just returned from the initiation and wanted to start his life with Maie. Dengg's arrival disturbed his plans. All the other young men had settled in after the initiation. They started building new houses, making new gardens, announcing their plans to pay the bride price, and some expected new additions to the family in the coming moons. He didn't want to take part in the *komba birr*. His issues remained unresolved, and the elders took their time to come up with a decision.

"I don't want to."

"What?" Kondai shot back. "You will do no such thing. Your father and his father before him all took part in this ceremony. I will be dead before you ever miss the *komba birr*, I don't want to hear anymore, go to Kamawagle tomorrow!"

"Ughhhh," he said, struggling to restrain himself.

Kondai turned around and returned to her house perturbed that Porugl would even think of such a thing as missing the *komba birr*. She shook her head and kept walking back to her house.

Porugl felt like smashing something. All he wanted was for the elders to make a decision. The leaders asked him about his choice, but he told them he didn't want to hurt either of the women, so he didn't want to choose one. Just when he thought the elders would call up the meeting and let them know their decision, they announced the *komba birr*. To him, the ceremony was another disturbance in the lead-up to making a decision by the elders.

The early morning mist was still lurking around the village the next day when Porugl left the *yal yungu*. His mother was right. He could not miss the *komba birr*. It will look bad on the family and on Kande Kumugl's name, he thought. He was not going to spoil his grandfather's legacy. He swiftly harvested all the red pandanus his father had planted for him. He prepared four bundles, one for himself and one each for his mother, Maie, and Dengg. As he walked past his mother's house, he called them to go and collect their bundles.

Waine met him along the way and they walked to the tribal meeting place. Some Akenku men had come earlier, and they milled around, grouping their *komba* bundles in the middle. Waine's bundle was smaller than all the bundles brought in. But Waine was just being Waine, so nobody bothered him.

"Do you think some beautiful Daneku girls will come?" asked Waine.

"What?"

"They said Daneku girls are really beautiful. I hope we get lucky," said Waine.

"We? You, Waine you, but I thought you are married."

"So, that doesn't stop me from taking part in the courting."

"I am not taking part in any courting, I have enough problems of my own," declared Porugl.

"Porugl, of all the young Akenku warriors, you cannot say this. If you do not take part, you will spoil your name for good."

"Waine, enough!"

"No, Porugl, you stop being a little girl. They have heard your story and there is a sizeable group of girls coming. They want to court with us, with you."

Waine was still persistent and didn't give him time.

"If you don't, then you will tarnish your name. Your father courted your mother, Kondai and won her over. The two women fighting at home, let them be. You didn't court them, they came on their own. People will say you didn't have the charm to bring home a woman after courting them and this tag will stick with you forever."

Porugl considered this for a moment.

"I can't and I won't," said Porugl.

"Are you scared you won't be able to live up to your father's name and Kande Kumugl's name? Is that it?" asked Waine.

"Waine!" shouted Porugl, "Just let me be."

"Alright."

"We will accommodate the Daneku tonight. They will leave tomorrow," announced Ormar to the enormous crowd of Akenku and Daneku villagers. "I welcome the young

Daneku women to Akenku. Tonight, you will court with young Akenku men."

The crowd roared in approval. On the previous occasion where the Akenku went to the Daneku village for the *amugl birr*, the young men from Daneku courted the Akenku girls.

Porugl had hoped the Daneku would take the *komba* and just leave. When Ormar confirmed the courting, he knew there would be pressure to take part. The young unmarried Akenku men didn't eat properly that evening. They left the *yal yungu* before the event started as the seasoned warriors watched in amusement. Older warriors stood watch at the edges of the village. Porugl dreaded this moment. His story had gone far and wide when he came out from the Underworld. Many of the young women in the surrounding villages wanted to come to Porugl, but when they heard of Maie and Dengg, they didn't. Girls from the Daneku village didn't know the situation, and they didn't bother. No young girl at the age of courting remained in Daneku. All of them made the trip to Gandia, home of the Akenku.

"Are you going to the courting tonight?" asked Dengg accusingly.

Maie saw Dengg talking to Porugl and quickly walked over. Neither woman gave any breathing space to the other. Maie told Waine not to worry when he tried to intercept her. Porugl left the two women and went with Waine

Each of the Akenku villagers took in a family from the Daneku. Maie and Dengg made sure Kondai chose a family that had no young girl. The last thing they needed was another one trying to come into Porugl's life. They pestered her about making sure Porugl didn't attend the courting.

"They are men, and whatever they do tonight is none of my business. I let Gamba do his thing, but he always came back to me," said Kondai kindly to the two women. "My dear husband, o how I miss him."

Tears formed in her eyes as she told Maie and Dengg about the first time Gamba courted her. Gamba had courted many women given his status as son of the great Kande Kumugl. Kondai doubted herself because many of the girls he courted exceeded in beauty. She succumbed and waited her turn. In her heart, she kept her mother's advice, who told her to be true to herself. This came to fruition when Gamba chose to marry her.

She told the two women that those words from her mother gave her strength. The first night of courting led to many more nights. Gamba forgot about all his other pursuits and continued to court Kondai. He finally chose to marry Kondai. Kondai asked Maie and Dengg if they had taken part in courting and they nodded. But now, they had forfeited that right to take part.

Young men and women prepared themselves for the night and put on their beads, feathers and painted their faces. They selected an old woman's house to host the event. Many of the young men congregated around the house. The young men became animated when the young Daneku women arrived in a long line with their mothers. The evening filled with the odor of their freshly oiled bodies and giggles as they passed by and entered the house. All the Daneku girls arrived with their mothers. They sat in a long line facing inwards towards the fireplace. The mothers sat in the corner of the house. Some sat near the fireplace.

"Akenku men, where are you, or are there no men in Gandia? These girls have come a long way. Maybe you are still boys. Where are the men of this land?" said one of the mothers, raising her voice.

"If you don't want to go in, we will," said one of the older warriors, who was there to keep an eye on them.

"I wouldn't mind a young bride," said another taunting the young men.

The mothers in the house started singing inside the house. They also had their faces painted. They would watch over their daughters and observe interactions during courting.

A confident young man from the Akenku tribe stepped inside. One of the mothers sat at the door guiding the young men as they entered to go and sit between two girls. She stopped them when every girl had a partner. The other boys waited their turn later in the night. The men faced outward and also had their faces painted. Some had short headdresses, while others stuck a single feather in their headdress. The lead young man started the singing and all the young men and women joined in a chorus of chants. They shook their heads and torsos from side to side while singing. The intensity of the shaking and head twisting increased when they sang the chorus. Right there and then, the men leaned back to the right, and the women leaned over and rubbed their noses. They then came up and leaned back to the left and rubbed noses with the woman on their left. The courting took a break after five songs. Girls who wanted to continue courting with the young men nudged them to stay. The rest stood up and made way for the other young people to enter.

One particular girl screened the young men for Porugl but didn't see him. She heard so much about him. His tale fascinated her. She thought of nothing else. There had been two breaks, and she released all the boys who courted her. She hoped he came in before the courting ended. She had spotted him earlier during the day and already made up her mind about him. She told her mother about this and her mother was at hand and would direct him to sit with her when he came in.

Porugl sat outside the *yal yungu* when Ormar came. The voices of the singing filled the air above. Ormar had been watching the courting with interest with all the other men and women.

"The *ambai kango* is going well. The Daneku girls have found some of our boys to be promising," he said to Porugl. "The Daneku will be happy to marry into Akenku. My mother was from Daneku."

Porugl nodded.

"I didn't see you there?"

"No," he said. He sighed.

"Porugl, look, I know you have this situation, but you have not married them yet. You are still free to take part. Have you ever taken part in *ambai kango*, or courting?"

Porugl shook his head.

"Ahh, my poor boy, you have to. It's what all young men experience and go through. Come, let's go, else you will regret it if you don't," insisted Ormar.

Porugl got up and followed Ormar. The young girl had told her mother during one of the breaks she wanted to court with Porugl, after not seeing him. The mother came out and told Ormar about it. The young girl's mother and Ormar had extended family relations. Ormar obliged and brought Porugl. Men, women and some children gathered around a couple of fires, listening to the singing inside and talking amongst themselves.

Occasionally, the people outside would say "*endomiwoho*," meaning 'it is gone' after a song had ended, complementing those who took part in the singing. The banter suddenly died down as Porugl made his way to the entrance of the house. He felt his stomach tremble. He had not taken part in any *ambai kango*, nor had any practice in the songs to be sung. He knew most of the songs, but he had never taken part in singing them because the occasion didn't present itself in the short time he was in Gandia. When he was small, he had watched courting take place, but had not taken part in any. He got bits and pieces of information from the stories that the elders and seasoned warriors told.

The chatter continued while the people kept their gaze on him. There was no line of waiting young men. All of them had their chance to court the girls from Daneku. The boys who remained were the ones whom the girls chose.

The others not selected went back to the *yal yungu* or stood around outside waiting for the courting session to end. Porugl felt guilty as he stood there. He had two women challenging each other at his home and here he was trying to get involved in courting. The last break was about to happen. Porugl recalled Ormar's words that this could be the only chance. He had to take part in *ambai kango* as an unmarried man. This thought stuck to his mind and so did Waine's words, which kept ringing in his head. Where is Waine? He thought.

"There is only one young man left," announced one of the mothers.

The anxious young girl glanced quickly at her mother. Was it Porugl? Please let it be him, she hoped in her heart. The courting couples stretched their legs and backs and got ready for the last session. The mother at the door beckoned him to enter and before she could direct him, the young girl's mother took his hand and led him to her daughter. He just followed, not knowing what to do or expect. The young men inside saw him enter, and they all felt energized again. The young girl made space for him to sit beside her. She stole a glance at him. He filled the doorway as he entered. The other girls also noticed the change in the atmosphere with his arrival. They all heard stories about him.

The young girl sensed a tingling sensation in her arms and legs, which shot right through into her body as his arms brushed hers. Her heart fluttered, releasing all sorts of emotions and making other places wet. For a moment, she was in a daze. The man of her dreams sat beside her, ready to court her. His body had an odor of the forest mixed with a manly scent.

The young girl's heart beat faster and making his heart increase its pace. He didn't expect this reaction from his own body. His senses became aware of the connection being established. Ormar didn't tell him her name, and it didn't matter. What mattered now was the feeling that engulfed him. She resonated with anticipation and he could feel every pulse coming from her. He had not touched a woman after coming out of the Underworld. Sweat drooled down his arms and a strong urge rose.

The lead young warrior sung the beginning of the chant and all the young men and women joined in unison. The crowd outside heard the difference in the sharp voices of the young women, which enveloped the strong voices of the young men. The interplay of tones teased each other and desired to linger on at the end of each verse. But the end also promised the onset of the next verse filled with emotion and drove the crescendo of voices high above the thatched roof of the old woman's house. The ether above welcomed the young voices and let it seep out further across the night sky. All houses still awake heard the singing and appreciated the promise it brought with it.

Porugl moved his body and swayed his head. He became one with everyone as their bodies moved in tandem. While some moved outwards, others moved inwards, complementing each other. The chorus came and at the signal of the lead singer; he leaned back really low to his right towards the young girl. At that moment, the young girl leaned over him and they both rubbed their noses. He could feel her breasts touch him. A mixture of oil and womanly body smells came strong to him, arousing his senses to heights he had never felt before. The elation he derived felt like nothing he experienced before. He closed his eyes and wanted to continue, but when the song hit the next part of the chorus; she got up and leaned back, rubbing noses with the other young man. Porugl rose up and leaned forward, this time over the girl on his other side, and they rubbed noses. The song ended and the next one started immediately. The lead singer kept the momentum going. Another wave of nose rubbing continued and every time he wanted it to continue with the particular young girl, it ended. This went on for many songs.

All the people crowded outside the entrance to get a glimpse of the courting. The enticing singing inside provoked some people outside to sing along. To old warriors and women listening, it brought back memories of when they had their first courting session. They got lost in their own thoughts while singing, swinging their heads and moving their torso. After the last song, all the mothers praised their daughters and the young men. The courting couples rose and stepped out into the cool air of the night. The people outside started leaving. Mothers stood not too close to their daughters but not too far away, watching their daughters talk briefly with their partners. Porugl stood there looking at this energetic young woman who had bright eyes. He smiled at her and she smiled back. He wanted to say something but couldn't find the words. Not that he couldn't muster something to say, but because he didn't want to create any false hopes. Despite how promising the courting had turned out to be, and the elation he had felt during the courting, he knew this was something that would never happen. The mother watched from a safe distance.

"That went really well," said Ormar walking to them.

Porugl breathed a sigh of relief after suffocating for a moment.

"My daughter, you made all of us feel young again with your singing," said Ormar to the young girl. "It is late. We can talk more tomorrow."

The young girl wanted to remain and talk some more with Porugl.

"Thank you for that," said Porugl to Ormar on their way back.

"I know," said Ormar, "Now we have to figure out how to deal with them tomorrow. Don't worry, I will handle this."

The whole Akenku tribe gathered at the meeting place the next morning. Daneku gathered on the other side of the meeting place. The first order of business was to do the speeches and present the *komba birr* to the Daneku. There was a loud wailing of appreciation as the Daneku received the big heap of *komba* from the Akenku. While the Daneku leaders distributed the *komba* amongst themselves, the family of two Daneku girls announced that they would remain. The men shouted a loud uproar of agreement and the women shouted in their special way called *aglang*. The families of the young men and women came together and embraced each other. Discussions heated up and middle men or *kakep* walked quickly in between the families to establish the bride price and timing. The young woman from Daneku courted by Porugl felt more and more depressed when she didn't see him in the crowd. She searched all the faces. Her mother saw her preoccupied mind. The mother knew her daughter wanted to stay. She had to make it known to Ormar. All the surrounding talking became inaudible because she had only one thing in mind. The mother moved closer to her and before she said anything, her daughter spoke.

"Mother, I want to stay."

"I know, but he is not here."

"I want to stay, tell Ormar, mother."

"Wait, I can see Ormar. Let me go and tell him."

Ormar saw the young girl's mother coming, and he knew he had to concoct something.

"We are getting worried, no sign?" said the mother to Ormar.

Ormar wanted to lie, but seeing the mother's face changed his mind.

"I am sorry, I should have told you already, the young man has two women at the house, we have not made a decision yet, it's my fault, he didn't want to go courting, I forced to him to, he really liked her, but we have not sorted out the situation here, I'm so sorry, he would have wanted her to stay."

A wave of disappointment swept over the mother's face.

"Ahh, they courted very well. You have said what needs to be said. We will be leaving shortly," said the mother.

The young girl turned her face away in tears when the mother told her about Porugl. Ormar stood there feeling depressed because he coerced Porugl to go courting. The Daneku left with words of gratitude to the Akenku tribe. No one saw the tears in her eyes. She covered her face with the leaves she placed on her head to carry the bundle of *komba*. Her legs walked, but her mind remained in Gandia. Porugl courted her. She wanted to just drop the bundle of *komba* and run back to Gandia. She was the last to be walking back to their village. Her mother stood along the path and occasionally waited for her to catch up. The young woman plodded along. One thing she knew, she was never going to court another man again.

6

The Decision

Dengg and Maie felt a sense of dread after the *komba birr*. Kondai showed no indication who she favored nor said anything that might give a hint of who she chose to remain. She treated both women equally and gave each of them equal amounts of time and affection. When she brought home food, she made sure the two women received the same quantity and quality. Everything she said contained 'Maie' and 'Dengg'. The two women noticed the small changes and gestures in her attitude. Both tried to get a spark in Kondai's eye, but she didn't show any to either of them. She only had the warmth of a mother, concerned that one of them would not be staying back. This made the two women even more anxious, and they tried harder to impress her. The two women forgot about being courteous and challenged each other over who knew more. A contentious issue occurred when they started discussing Kande Kumugl's family history.

Kondai hoped the discussion would not go there, but

it did. Each woman making her claim that she knew more than the other. Both women didn't know the story behind Porugl's name. Kondai figured that if one of them mentioned the reason behind Porugl's name, she would tell the elders herself who she chose to remain back. But both Dengg and Maie didn't know. Nonetheless, Kondai enjoyed listening to the two women. They even knew about Yal Wai and his travel from the south to Gandia.

"I heard Kande Kumugl's grandfather was the first of the ancestors to be laid at the ancestral grounds on Bindekai," said Dengg

"Do you know his name?" asked Maie

"Okun Kumugl," said Dengg confidently.

"It's Gotndagl," replied Maie sharply. "Okun Kumugl is Kande Kumugl's father. His grandfather's name is Gotndagl Kumugl."

Maie felt pleased. She had scored precious points against Dengg.

It surprised Kondai that Maie knew Kande Kumugl's grandfather. Most people didn't know a lot about him. Gamba may have mentioned it. Kande Kumugl, while blessing the baby Porugl, a day after his birth recalled that he and his father with a few men brought a dying Gotndagl from the Porugl Mountains to the new lands of Gandia.

Dengg fumed. If she didn't score any points right now, it would be over. Kondai would definitely select Maie. Her mind raced to find a peculiar piece of information that would throw Maie off her game. Kondai's facial reaction proved that Maie was leading at the moment. But it was not over. The game had only begun and Dengg had to search deep into her memory.

"My grandmother was a young girl when Kande Kumugl's grandfather was laid to rest" said Dengg and didn't want to give any credibility to Maie by calling 'Gotndagl Kumugl's name.

This aroused Kondai's interest.

"Your grandmother was an Akenku woman?" asked Kondai.

"Yes," said Dengg, smiling brightly. "We have bloodlines here," and mentioned the name of an Akenku warrior who had relations with Dengg's family.

"I never knew that," said Kondai and smiled at Dengg.

That's it, thought Dengg. I am back in the game.

Maie cringed. It appalled Maie that Dengg should find some distant and vague fact about her grandmother to bring as an issue of argument.

"That's interesting," said Maie in a sarcastic manner." What's her name?"

Dengg had to defend her victory for the moment and quickly called a name that came from the top of her head. It sounded fake and Maie wanted to laugh. Kondai said nothing and nodded her head. The two women nearly fisted each other when they talked about Dingan.

"I saw Dingan's uncle at the *komba birr* with some other people from the Wakiku tribe. He was staring at you, Kondai. He must have sensed someone looking at him and when he turned around to see me looking at him, he quickly avoided my gaze," said Maie.

"What?" said Kondai. "What business did he have here?"

"Kondai, you have to be careful. From now on, I will go around with you all the time, we don't want this evil man to do anything," said Dengg.

"Porugl will deal with him if he tries anything," said Maie.

"Maie, what if Kondai is going to the gardens, and attacked there? What if they ambush her there?" said Dengg.

"And why would he do such a thing?" asked Maie

"Because Porugl killed his nephew," Dengg yelled.

"You were not here when Porugl killed Dingan, so shut up!"

"No you shut up, you have no concern for Kondai's life!"

"Enough, the both of you," said Kondai in a loud voice.

Both women stood up with their fists clenched.

"I can take care of myself. I took care of myself when Porugl was in the endless pit. I can take care of myself now," she said.

None of them said anything, and they sat lost in their thoughts. Dengg felt victorious, and Maie continued to breathe heavily as she stared into the fire. Porugl's indecision angered Kondai. He should be here to make up his own mind. This thought made her want to scream at the top of her lungs. She still found it difficult to favor one over the other. A marriage with Dengg from the Kumoku tribe would be strategic, paving the way to end tribal tensions and differences. The implications of such a marriage would be huge. Even though many marriages existed between Akenku and Kumoku, the two tribes still engaged in war over the generations, nonetheless. A marriage between Porugl and Dengg would bring the two tribes so much closer together and be a first step to end the animosity between them. After living with Dengg for many moons, Kondai came to understand her way of thinking. She was the firstborn and she acted and talked the part. She should have been born a man.

Maie, on the other hand, was full of kindness and compassion. She often thought about this considerate young woman during her pregnancy with Dingan's child. Maie had only gentle words and a beautiful smile. She couldn't forget Maie and her personality. She was always courteous and genuine. Kondai felt sorry for her because she did change a bit. Kondai had never seen Maie angry until Dengg came. Maie had a temper and showed it during the confrontation.

From that night onwards, Maie and Dengg hated each other intensely. This dislike usually disguised in front of Kondai started becoming evident. The two women berated each other openly. Kondai became entrenched in the crossfire. The intensity of the exchanges went to new heights when Porugl came to visit. Even when Porugl was relieving himself, both women would be nearby, one keeping an eye on the other. The three of them went everywhere together. To the gardens in the mountains, to the river, to gatherings, they went everywhere together. Porugl often wondered when the two women relieved themselves. Kondai watched in amusement as the folly continued and played out in front of her. But she also felt sad knowing that one of them would leave. Kondai spoke to Dengg and Maie the night before the day of the announcement.

"My two daughters, the time has come to make a decision. My heart pains as I speak to you."

Tears formed in Kondai's eyes.

"Unfortunately, I don't know what to do. The elders will come tomorrow and tell us. Whatever the outcome tomorrow, both of you will still be like daughters to me," she said and stepped out of the hut so they would not see her cry.

An uncomfortable silence loomed in the hut. Both Maie and Dengg sat at the fireplace at either ends. Dengg felt anger rising within her. I come from a respectable family. Definitely, the elders will chooses me or else, Porugl, his mother and his tribe will be making a great mistake. I'm not going to lose out to an ordinary girl like Maie. Everyone knows my family. It is in Porugl's best interests and his tribe for him to marry me, she thought.

Maie tried to understand everything that had happened so far. Why did she have to comfort a helpless pregnant woman many moons ago? She thought. All this would not have happened if she minded her own business. She recalled the first time she met Kondai. From a distance, she saw Kondai standing on the edge of a cliff very late in her pregnancy. It was the second such occasion where she saw this woman at the exact spot, most probably thinking of stepping over.

She let her mother walk ahead and remained back to meet this pregnant woman at the point where the two paths met. She made sure to pace herself so they could meet at the junction. Kondai was startled to see Maie and didn't make any effort to hide the fact that she had been crying. Tears still streamed down her face.

Maie took the bag from Kondai's head and saw Kondai's swollen legs. The walking made it worse. Her bag contained scrawny looking sweet potatoes and withered garden vegetables. The two walked along the main track until they reached the part where it led to Kondai's hut. Maie did some cleaning in and around the hut. Kondai went inside and rested. Maie heard her breathing heavily and left.

When Kondai woke up, she immediately thought about the young girl she met. What a delightful girl, she thought. From that time on, Maie and Kondai met occasionally. She told Maie about all the events leading to her being pregnant and about Porugl. She believed he was not dead.

Everyone across the lands heard Porugl's story of being thrown down into the endless pit. Maie knew no one ever came back. She felt empathy for Kondai. During one of her visits, Kondai gave birth to the still-born child. In a fit of rage Dingan wanted to kill Kondai when a young muscular man disturbed him. She watched in horror as the two men struggled against each other. Maie saw the young man behead the notorious Dingan Kumugl. No one else saw the beheading except Kondai, Dingan's aunty, and herself. Kondai felt weak with all the stress and loss of blood and passed out. Maie remained with Kondai to comfort her.

The bright morning of the next day could not uplift the sense of dread that hung over everyone. Parents and relatives came to witness the event. The elders, including Ormar huddled together deep in conversation. Kondai sat by herself, not wanting to show any affiliation. Young warriors from Porugl's tribe idled around. Then one of the elders cleared his throat and began.

"Good morning to all families from across the river and the mountains. Thank you for coming."

The elder appreciated Maie's arrival and then Dengg. The elder explained the difficulty in taking a stand because both Maie and Dengg had proven beyond a reasonable doubt they had traits that the tribe found attractive. The elder thanked both families for raising two beautiful, hardworking women. Another elder rose up and said that even Porugl found it difficult to make a decision. Some impatient family members uttered to the elders to get on with it.

"We also feel this cannot be dragged on any further and have made a decision. We have decided for Maie to stay, for the only reason that Maie came here before Porugl came out from the Underworld." The elder paused and looked towards Maie and asked, "We have decided, what say you?"

"I want to stay," said Maie, holding back her joy.

Dengg didn't take her eyes off the elder. The elder felt Dengg's sharp gaze and ended his oration. In a rage of discomfort and hurt, she let out a wild shriek and ran away from the meeting area. Her family members followed suit fearing she would do something drastic like taking her own life. Her father remained disappointed with the decision. The elders then came forth and brought what they had as parting gifts to compensate Dengg for her time. Ormar brought his choicest pig and made a show of it in front of Kondai.

Dengg became hysterical near the river which ran beside Kondai's hut. Her mother kept a vigilant eye on her.

"There are many young men who are leaders still out there," she said.

"But none of them are Porugl," she screamed back at her mother.

In her life, no one rejected her. All the young boys in the surrounding villages brawled to court her, ever since she came of age to be courted. She only allowed boys from the lineage of chiefs to court her, and she flirted with them because of her beauty. The boys would do anything for her. At one time, Dengg's mother made a casual remark that she needed more cuscus fur. Dengg related this to a certain boy. The next day, there was a long line of cuscus tied to poles outside Dengg's house. It shocked Dengg's mother. She made sure she would have a good word about this boy to Dengg's father. Many of Dengg's uncles also benefitted as the young men's family made sure to keep them happy.

Dengg had brothers after her, but they didn't have the

erect stature and height as Dengg. She grew up thinking like a firstborn and acted the part. When she heard of Porugl, it dawned on her that she had to be married to him. Getting married to Porugl would bring more prestige to her family and ease her father's thoughts. Dengg knew her father had wished her to be a boy. To make up for that, she would marry into the tribe of a well-known family and what better way to do so than to marry Porugl, grandson of the great Kande Kumugl, incumbent heir to the Akenku chieftaincy. Marrying him would be the pinnacle of all marriages, she thought.

When that didn't turn out the way she envisioned, all her pride and ambition seeped out instantly. The people would see her as just another girl in the village. She resented the decision and hated the elder who made the announcement. When her uncles tried to soothe her and called the name of the young man who had been in pursuit of her, she yelled back at her uncles and swore at them. She kept sitting on one of the rocks near the river, not heeding any of the calls from her family to return home.

As the river surged forth, thoughts and emotions began forming in her mind. Evil and dark thoughts took hold of her. The more she thought about it, the more it became clear what she had to do. Nothing could solace her other than the evil she conjured up. She felt better thinking these evil thoughts, and she savored all of them. The pain she felt entered her heart, and it struck her. The only way to appease her pain and suppress her anger and embarrassment was revenge.

"Revenge, yes, that is the only way," whispered the surrounding air.

She turned around quickly but saw no one. This thread of thought gripped her.

"Porugl, Maie, and the Akenku tribe will pay for it," she uttered to herself.

"Yes, all of them will pay dearly and painfully," came the silent whisper in the light breeze that passed her.

She turned around again, but it was just the wind.

"You cannot allow this rejection to overcome you, death to the Akenku, that is the only way to save your face and that of your father, they disrespected him and made a fool of him in front of all the tribes, you have to save his face," said the strange whispers in the wind.

"What, who is that?" she said, looking around.

"There is only one cure for your pain," the voices kept coming.

"Mother, is that you?"

Dengg's mother came to her.

"Let's go home," said her mother.

"Death to Porugl, death to Maie, death to all Akenku," she whispered aloud.

"What did you say?" asked her mother.

Tears rolled down her face, thinking of her father. Why me? She thought. Why couldn't I have been born a man? Why was I born a woman? She screamed a ferocious scream.

Relatives nearby came running and saw her mother

soothing her. Other beings also heard the scream.

Gurr-toki, Kimin-ege and Agandua rejoiced. They danced around the river and the marshes. Their silent whispers into Dengg's ears worked. It had not been easy searching for a worthy adversary after Porugl survived the treacherous currents of Sikewake. News of Porugl's escape stunned the ancient serpent after seeing him engulfed in the raging foam of the three rivers crashing into each other. Initially, the minions believed Dingan, being a fierce warrior, would do the job. He had already murdered Gamba, Porugl's father. He then did the unthinkable by forcing himself on Gamba's wife and impregnating her and forcefully took over as Chief of Akenku. Kerwanba knew this would end up in the way she thought. Even the minions spoke proudly that they had found the perfect enemy.

But Porugl killed Dingan. The reports shocked the Underworld and the tag 'Son of the Underworld' broke out in all the realms. Every being and creature wanted to relate to him. Kewand Kumugl got a lot of attention being the boy's mentor. Goglko told many creatures and beings that he and Porugl had shared smoke. Many beings knew the *makan nem* lived a solitary life and thought this as unbelievable. Nondo didn't go out of his abode with Milime as often as he used to. But during the few times he did, he would detail how he healed Porugl from the life-threatening injuries he sustained from his fall into the pit. Nondo didn't mention that Porugl gave him the *gwika* leaf. The Underworld heard Porugl's account of snatching the gwika leaf out from a group of angry dwarves. As far as the Underworld knew, Porugl still had the *gwika* leaf.

The more time the minions took to search for a worthy adversary, the more Kerwanba became agitated. Coercing Dingan's three half-brothers from Kande Kumugl's other wives seemed to be a last resort as options ran out. When that ended fatally for the half-brothers, Kerwanba barred the minions from entering the Underworld until they found someone with enough reason to kill Porugl. While Kerwanba went through her mind about how she would deal with him, the Underworld went into a frenzy. This obsession the Underworld had with him infuriated Kerwanba. Her brown fiery eyes now burned red with rage.

Every household the minions visited, every gathering and every conversation they overheard had nothing but positive comments for Porugl. Even the surrounding enemy tribes spoke with awe and fear of Porugl. No one had strong intentions to end Porugl's life anytime soon. They searched far and wide, listened to every gossip and utterance. They studied every facial twitch and emotion of the people in Gandia and the surrounding villages.

All that changed when Dengg appeared on the scene. At first, the minions thought nothing of it. Women came and went in men's lives. They paid little attention to the strain building up in Porugl's house until they realized the fierce competition between both women to remain as his wife. Dengg had the character to pull off what the Minions had in mind. They started to plant seeds of hate and malice in both women's hearts and minds. The dislike grew each day, and the minions incited Deng and Maie to detest each other. In front of Kondai, both of them exhibited a persona of calm and love. But they hated each other.

"She is the daughter of a 'nobody'. You are the daughter of a chief. You are bound to marry Porugl," the minions whispered into Dengg's ear.

"She didn't witness Porugl killing Dingan, you did because you are his rightful wife," the minions breathed into Maie's mind.

This carried on day and night until the appointed day. The minions eagerly waited to see how it played out. And sure enough, to their utmost delight, the elders chose Maie. The Minions agreed Dengg had the character to follow through with what they had in mind. If no man in all the land had a strong will to kill Porugl, then it had to be a woman. The next part of their evil scheme went into motion when they saw her running towards the river in tears. Finally, reporting to Kerwanba didn't seem scary anymore. They felt pleased and excited.

"Minions!" thundered Kerwanba.

The minions scurried to her.

"What is this I hear?" she bellowed.

"O queen of the deep dark, we have found our adversary, a woman," said Kimin-ege

Kerwanba murmured something in her sleep. She seemed different. The events at the cliffs of Sikewake affected the serpent, and she didn't sleep well. The vibrations from mentioning Porugl's name came like a sharp rock pricking her and caused her to stir, even in her deepest sleep. Later, the realms would learn that she had bitten the creature or being who called Porugl's name. The bite injected her poisonous venom into the victim, causing pain for a lifetime.

The minions had been with Kerwanba ever since they came into being and understood their purpose. They maintained her authority across all the realms and reported everything they saw and heard. They caught anything Kerwanba missed. She kept a tight rule. The realms didn't have any problems with her. The *yokond* or dwarf realm, the *makan nem* realm, the spirit or *gigl* realm, the evil spirit or *kangi* realm, and many more; all yielded to Kerwanba as the supreme authority. Then humans came tumbling down the sinkhole. A few survived and allowed to dwell there. But Porugl's arrival set irrevocable changes to life beneath the earth.

The humans didn't have a realm in the Underworld. The Underworld understood that the few humans who came down the pit existed because Kerwanba allowed it. But Porugl had gone beyond her authority. His escape was an act of defiance and a challenge to Kerwanba's authority. This was an action unheard of in all the realms.

Kerwanba shifted. She thought that culling Porugl's first-born son, a half-ling from Dikamb, his *gigl ambu* wife, would have controlled them. The minions reported that the creatures and beings in that realm became more vocal. They expressed their thoughts and ideas freely and supported Porugl. Their affinity to disregard Kerwanba's wishes grew and other realms took notice. They had opinions on how life in the Underworld should be or would be without the serpent. These ideas flowed freely, something which would have been unheard of previously. They no longer hid their concerns and discussed it amongst themselves and allowed these ideas to filter into all the other realms. The threat that Kerwanba posed was of no consequence anymore, as these views gained prominence in other realms.

Kerwanba and her minions did not pick up any murmur or whisper in the other realms yet. They focused their attention on the realm that Porugl lived in. The minions told her that if this continued, they would reject her rule in her domain.

Initially, she thought that an increasing human population in her domain would put her authority to the test. She had a long history with humans before, and during the Kundawii, and knew their natural tendencies. It turned out that it was not the humans who were instigating this build-up of thought against her, but the dwellers of her domain, a place she established with her authority. She came down here after the bloodbath of the Kundawii to maintain the balance. No one knew the great secret she harbored that forced her to live beneath the earth. She had feared the curious nature of humans to start digging out her history. But now, her own subjects were questioning her authority. Porugl's action had set an example. She had to stub out any glorious notion of rebellion before it blew out of proportion.

"Good, good, and did you start work on her?"

"Already oh mighty queen of the deep dark," said Gurr-toki.

"You have done well, my children."

The minions knew better than to jump for joy or feel emotionally comfortable. She had the habit of changing her mood in an instant. They kept their elation at bay. For now, they had avoided being bitten. Their confidence and determination egged them more than ever to continue work on Dengg.

A sudden thought occurred to Kerwanba while the minions waited for their next orders. The serpent had found an opening to plot her devious scheme.

"I will make him pay for humiliating me. I will show them who I am. He will suffer a slow and painful death."

7

The Tambaiku Tribe

U nder Kerwanba's vehement orders, Kimin-ege, Gurr-
toki and Agandua increased their task on Dengg
every night. They barraged her thoughts and infiltrated
her mind. In her dreams, the minions planted false visions
of healing and acceptance. They whispered into her ears
how she would redeem herself and the shame she endured
from the rejection. They reminded her that no man would
pursue her like they did previously. People laughed at her
back and gossiped about her intensely, they told her. The
minions pressed on deep into her sub-conscious that people
suspected her of being a *kumo kwimbo*, or a witch; the reason
for her rejection.

"Me, a witch?" she stuttered and woke up in the middle
of the night sweating and breathing hard.

They went further and lied into her ear that the rejection
blocked her womb. She would bear no children. In order for

that curse to be reversed, she had to kill Porugl. The minions continuously whispered to her that all men of the land knew about this.

"Your revenge must be war, for your sake and your father. You need a strong ally, you need a powerful ally," the minions pressed on.

Night after night, they continually drummed these messages into her head and sub-conscious until it became unbearable for her. She could not sleep because all these voices kept on ringing in her head. When she closed her eyes, she saw Maie and Porugl. She had no quiet moment. This continued for many days up to a point where Dengg felt like exploding. That's when she made up her mind.

Dengg left early one morning. She met Dee Kumugl in a secret place near a cave opening. Dengg had made eyes to Dee Kumugl the previous day, and informed him that she wanted to meet him at this particular place. Dee Kumugl didn't object. He had always desired Dengg from the first day he saw her. But he couldn't do anything because men and women from the same tribe didn't have relationships. His mother had seen the young man's attitude towards Dengg on many occasions and warned him about it.

"What I see in your eyes doesn't belong there," she said.

"My eyes?" asked Dee.

"Yes, your eyes. They should not be looking at places where it cannot stay."

"Mother, what are my eyes doing?"

She nodded towards Dengg, who walked past them.

"What, you think…"

"Just stop this nonsense. You know it will never happen. She is your sister."

Upon hearing this, Dee walked off angrily, because his infatuation with Dengg was visible to his mother. Maybe his mother knew about their relationship.

"Did anybody see you?" asked Dengg

"No, no one saw me and you?" replied Dee.

"It doesn't matter. I wanted to tell you that this must stop."

"You called me here to tell me this?" asked Dee.

She then told Dee Kumugl, chief of Kumoku, why she had to marry the old and aging Bindi Kumugl of the Tambaiku. Dengg explained that the marriage to the old chief would ensure a powerful ally who would respond to his call when he went to war with the Akenku.

"Why should we go to war with Akenku?"

"Listen, you haven't matured yet. You are still thinking like a child."

The minions watched eagerly as Dengg weaved her magic of words.

"You became chief after your father, Kogun Kumugl, died, but you will never be a man of your own. Your father and his fathers before never really came out and stood up to the great Akenku. Now is the time to declare war on the Akenku because they have no leader and remain fractured. Don't be a small boy and let the Tambaiku do your dirty work for you."

The words stung Dee Kumugl and all his erotic feelings towards Dengg disappeared. Dee Kumugl had inherited a generation of belittlement by the Akenku. Dengg convinced him that if he didn't respond to the times, he would just be another man trying to get out of the shadows of the Akenku.

"You will just be as insignificant as your father," the minions whispered into his ear.

"You are insignificant like your father," Dengg told Dee Kumugl.

"Take the challenge and uphold your father's name. For once, you have the opportunity to restore the name and pride of Kumoku," the minions whispered.

Dee Kumugl's deep thoughts brought him back home. He had experienced men deriding his father the chief, even men from his own tribe. For many generations, the Akenku outclassed the Kumoku in warfare and in all other tribal matters. Dengg had stated a fact. Though he prided himself as chief of the Kumoku, it gave him no comfort as he knew the difficult task ahead. The thoughts of history repeating itself emerged when the land heard Porugl had come out from the Underworld. His father and his father before him had all been known to accede to the might and glamour of the Akenku tribe.

One fine day, I will attack Akenku without notice and they will pay for all the misery they caused us, he thought. And now, the opening presented itself. It didn't come from a warrior or elder, but a young, beautiful woman. The sacrifice for the greatness of his tribe overwhelmed his desire for her.

He would not walk in the shadow of Akenku nor anyone, least of all Porugl.

Dee made the arrangement without informing Dengg's father. By the time her father knew, the Tambaiku had already travelled to Dawake, the Kumoku village, to receive their bride and pay the bride price. Seeing the young girl aroused Bindi Kumugl feelings he thought no longer existed. He would do anything for this beautiful young bride.

The Akenku paid no attention to the bridal ceremony between Dengg and Bindi Kumugl. They saw a distraught young woman eager to restore respect to herself and her family marrying quickly to an old chief.

"Poor girl," the Akenku villagers said.

"She comes from a good family. Why did the elders reject her?" asked another.

"Who knows, she wanted a chief, now she got one, it's hilarious," said another, and they laughed.

"This Bindi Kumugl, Chief of Tambaiku, I don't really know much about him," stated one Akenku villager. "The Tambaiku are so far away. How did this happen?"

Ormar overheard the villagers, and it bothered him. If the young girl wanted to restore her name and that of her family, she would have easily married into the surrounding tribes. But she went to a tribe so far away. The cold climate restricted other tribes from venturing into the land of the Tambaiku. Other tribes knew little of their customs and traditions. The Tambaiku didn't come down into the lower lands. He made a mental note and sought the counsel of the elders.

"Yes, the young girl we rejected has married the old chief Bindi Kumugl of the Tambaiku," responded one of the elders to Ormar.

"They have been taking lands by force," added another elder.

"Maybe the Kumoku are trying to gain their favor through this marriage," said another elder.

"Looks that way," said the first elder.

The Akenku heard the commotion across the river as the Kumoku welcomed the Tambaiku into Dawake village. A long line of pigs followed the Tambaiku. The main group hoisted shells and other items on a long bamboo pole. They arrived after traveling for three days. Bindi Kumugl dressed in his best attire and his enthusiasm protruded before him. The Kumoku women wailed in their special way called aglang and the men received the Tambaiku with shouting and victorious chants.

Dengg put Bindi Kumugl to task during their first night as man and wife. She reminded herself of the pain and embarrassment as the old man went on top of her. She stopped him midway.

"Hey what are you doing?" yelled the chief.

"I know, wait, and tell me this."

"What is it?"

"You have to go to war with the Akenku. They say Porugl, grandson of Kande Kumugl, is the greatest warrior in all of Kondaland. Is he the greatest, my chief?" she said.

"The greatest warrior, huh? Ok we will see about that."

He could have any woman he wanted, but this beautiful young girl came to him out of her freewill, he thought. If going to war with Akenku made her happy, then that's what he would do. He feared no one. The land in the north knew of him and his tribe. They had a reputation of being ferocious in battle and he had a secret weapon. A weapon so terrible and powerful, no other tribe could suppress. Surrounding villages watched petrified as he unleashed his secret weapon into battle. He did wonder if his name and fame equaled that of Kande Kumugl because word of Kande Kumugl's greatness travelled the length and breadth of Kondaland.

Bindi Kumugl rested, satisfied, and relaxed. Sleep came to him quickly, sending him off into bliss. The minions giggled to themselves, watching what unfolded as a result of their coercion. They increased the intensity on Bindi Kumugl. Kerwanba had warned them that if they failed, she would bite them. The minions knew it was better to be dead than to live after being bitten by the ancient serpent. They watched with satisfaction as Dengg brought the old man into agreement. The minions started their work when the old chief went into a deep sleep.

"We thought you were great," whispered Kimin-ege.

"But maybe Kande Kumugl is greater than you," continued Gurr-toki

"Porugl is here, he is just a boy, and he cannot be greater than you, or is he?" Agandua breathed into his mind.

"Your son Dongam is weak, its time you had another son," teased Kimin-ege into the sleepy mind of Bindi Kumugl.

The minions watched gleefully as the old Bindi Kumugl, chief of the Tambaiku, murmured to himself in his sleep.

"Remember, you have the greatest secret weapon. Who can be against you?" the minions pressed on into his sub-conscious.

"Maybe Porugl will marry your beautiful young bride after he destroys you. After all he slept with her already before you," whispered Kimin-ege into the deepest part of Bindi Kumugl's sub-conscious.

"Never," shouted the old man. He woke up.

His breathing took time to subside as Dengg lay peacefully. A sudden urge of jealousy swept over him. She is mine and mine alone; he thought. I will teach this imbecile a lesson, I will give something nice to the Akenku, something to think about.

8

The Ambush

"Porugl, Porugl," a voice called out.

"Go and see who it is," murmured Maie.

He waited to hear the voice again. The birds tweeted through the crisp air in the early morning light. Porugl built a new house for Maie beside Kondai's hut. He and Maie had mastered the art of secret signals and Maie already knew when to expect Porugl just by the twitch of his mouth or actions from his hand. The casual observer didn't understand the meaning of the normal gestures in everyday life. But to both of them, they had a completely different meaning.

"Porugl," the voice called again, this time louder.

The cool morning air greeted him with freshness as he stepped out. Porugl's senses heightened, and he held his axe steady beside him. This place had both fond and terrible memories. Someone ran to him. He looked around. The last time people ran to him here, they bound and gagged and threw him down into the endless pit. He kept his gaze on the person running towards him. A small boy arrived beckoning Porugl to follow him. In between his gasps for air, the small boy informed him of an urgent meeting at the *yal yungu* and the elders called every warrior to come at once. Porugl didn't respond. His grip was still on the axe. The small boy saw his posture and drew back. In a calm tone, the small boy told him why the elders requested his presence. Apparently, a confrontation occurred with the Kumokus.

Kondai and Maie came out to see Porugl and the young boy turning the bend. Kondai looked up to the peaks of Bindekai, still covered in the morning mist.

She called out to the ancestors, saying, "You brought him to me, take care of him."

The river beside their hut gushed fervently and the first streaks of sunlight streamed through Bindekai and hit the land. Maie struggled to contain her disappointment at seeing him leave. Grudgingly, she followed Kondai to the garden and started planting fresh, sweet potatoes.

Strange gossip circulated amongst the women folk right after the bridal ceremony between Bindi Kumugl and Dengg took place. One woman heard from another that the Kumoku started this alliance with the Tambaiku for something big. And that the Tambaiku came with all sorts of dark rituals and magic from their cold lands. Other women also heard the story and pointed out that Tambaiku had a secret weapon, a weapon so grotesque no other tribe could withstand. They said Akenku had to be prepared. Kondai knew an enemy started its campaign by using the woman to spread fear through gossip. This never happened during Kande Kumugl's reign. He came from the old school of thought and stopped mediums that spread fear like gossip. He would have cut out the women's tongues or have their husbands do it in front of the tribe. Things changed and such standards forgotten since his death.

The elders and young and seasoned warriors all stood outside the *yal yungu* deep in conversation when Porugl came. They welcomed him and the young warriors stood aside. Like his grandfather, he was tall and solidly built. His broad shoulders and muscular arms complemented his large feet and sturdy legs. Ormar suggested they move into the *yal yungu* and begin. Each found a space to sit while others stood towards the edges of the *yal yungu*. The elders all sat near the central fireplace.

"We had a quarrel with the Kumoku, which could have resulted in a skirmish," said Ormar.

He called one of the elders to explain what had happened.

"Our womenfolk were going to their gardens when a Kumoku war party tried to drag one of the girls away. The women screamed for help and luckily, some of our young warriors rescued her."

There was silence in the *yal yungu*.

"The enemy war party hurled insults at our tribe and at Kande Kumugl, after they crossed the river," continued the elder.

Porugl's eyes widened and those near him heard his teeth grinding.

"Under normal circumstances, we would have gone to war with the Kumoku, but right now our tribe is... unsteady—"

"We can beat them any time," cut in one of the young warriors in a strong voice.

A loud roar of approval lifted the roof of the *yal yungu*. Kondai heard it, as did many Akenku women. Porugl felt his blood circulating faster as many of the men tried to speak at the same time.

"Quiet," shouted Ormar.

He explained to the warriors that they beat Kumoku in every battle and would still beat them. They had acted without provocation. He wanted to know their true intentions.

Since Dingan's death, Ormar had taken the role of lead spokesman for the tribe. He displayed skills as a tough and smart negotiator, able to suppress the vile anger of his warriors. Lingering at the back of his mind, he knew the Akenku could not go into battle without a chief. He didn't want to state this explicitly as it might make the tribe think he wanted to be chief. Despite the long and glorious history of the Akenku chieftaincy, recent events embroiled the institution in treachery, dishonor, and blood. He didn't want to have any part of that.

"We will ask them to explain their actions and then demand compensation for this intrusion. If they act in any other way, then we will respond with aggression," he said.

"But first, I want to know if you did anything to make the Kumoku act like this?"

There was silence as every warrior looked around.

"One thing is for sure; we will not let the Kumoku get away with this. If we do, they will continue. We will put a stop to this once and for all," said Ormar.

Some of the young warriors felt dismayed by his statement, but did not argue.

One of them said, "If they don't respond, we will attack."

"We will kill them all," said the young warrior whose sister the Kumoku had tried to abduct.

Kupme, the village handyman, brought the message across the river to the Dawake village, giving the Kumoku one day to respond. The warriors stayed around the *yal yungu*. Some made a mental note to add more arrows to their quiver. Others checked their bowstrings and sharpened their war axes.

"What do you think will happen?" Waine asked Porugl.

"I don't know. We will wait and see."

"It's been a while since we fought them. You were still in the Underworld. No one died, but we burnt some of their houses down."

"That could be the reason."

"But who cares? We have Porugl and his everlasting bow," announced Waine proudly into the air.

Porugl smiled and shook his head.

"That reminds me, we have to make another quiver of arrows for ourselves, just to be sure," said Waine.

Then a familiar face walked towards Porugl. He got a shock of his life to see Ningir. The two embraced and wept.

"When did you come?" said Porugl

"Yesterday," said Ningir.

"And mother?"

"We both came."

Ningir was Porugl's cousin. He and his mother ran away when, Dingan, killed Sie his father right after he killed Gamba. Porugl noticed that he also had his ears and nose pierced and hugged him again, glad to have his blood relative come back. Ningir and his mother spent many seasons in Daneku village and came back when they heard Porugl had returned. They would have all gone to Kondai's house to celebrate Ningir's return, but the looming confrontation meant they remained in the *yal yungu*.

The one-day period passed and everyone moved about with expectation. Women and children went to their gardens in the morning and got all chores done before midday. The men all gathered at the *yal yungu* discussing the different scenarios.

"Not all the young warriors will accompany us to the meeting place. You know where to station yourselves at points on the mountain range to keep an eye on the land. Another group will flank us along the river. Seasoned warriors will lead our tribe to the common ground to receive our compensation demands. The elders and women and children will follow from a distance," said Ormar.

"Every warrior must have a full quiver of arrows," said another elder. "This is not a peace ceremony. We have demanded compensation, so be ready."

Warriors took out their quivers of arrows hung in the ceiling of the *yal yungu*. They brought out their longer war axes. They painted their face and bodies in black ash. Some made patterns on their face with white limestone powder. Everyone wore a headdress made of cassowary feathers, which covered their face making every warrior look dark and menacing.

The warriors marveled at Porugl's bow when he brought it out of the *yal yungu*. The sleek structure of the bow emanated both grace and power. The bow stood taller than the rest due to Porugl's height. When he blew away the dust that had settled, they saw the elegance of craftsmanship that brought such a creation into life. It had a personality of its own and spoke to all the warriors. From one end to the other, the smooth contour of both the bow and bowstring indicated that every shot would be accurate and deadly. Porugl pulled the bowstring to test it. The vibration that followed told the warriors that this was no ordinary bow.

A sense of pride filled Waine, seeing the glances Porugl's bow received. He held his bow close and looking at it said," Don't worry, you are doing fine."

One of the elders approached Porugl.

"I won't be needing this anymore, my son. I have stood in battle many times with your grandfather. I now join the last line of defense. I am proud to give you this."

All around, the warriors saw the exchange. Porugl stood up and hugged the old man. At that moment, Ormar spoke with a great voice across the Kumoku lands.

"All peoples around and in the land, we, the Akenku, are coming to the Kumoku to receive your explanation of how you tried to abduct one of our daughters. You have erred and for this you will compensate the Akenku."

Then all Akenku warriors in their traditional war cry shouted at the top of their voices. Far away villages heard the war cry. Surrounding hamlets around the periphery of Gandia all heard it. Again and again they heard the war cry ring across the skies. Women moved frantically and children told to be quiet as a deathly resonance hovered over the land. Elders ran the different scenarios in their minds. No one knew what the outcome would be.

"The warrior's mind must not be distracted in the time of war," the elders repeated. "Do not think about your wife. If you die in battle, she will marry your brother, so don't think about her. What belongs to the tribe stays in the tribe."

"Don't think about your children. The land has blessed you with them and to the tribe they belong. If you live, you see them grow. If you die, they carry your name on in the tribe," continued another elder. "All you young warriors, especially the recent initiates, show us you are a man, or are you just a woman in a man's body? What's that penis for then? Prove to us you are a man."

At hearing this, the young warriors looked for objects to smash their fists with. Porugl got up and, with clenched fists, landed one solid punch on the trunk of a young tree. The tree nearly dislodged itself from the ground as its green leaves flung up into the air. The elders and seasoned warriors heard thuds as young warriors vented their power on any object they could find. The elders saw his strength and gasped.

"Do not think about your father or your mother. They have lived their lives. You have to live yours," the elders continued.

"The first man who comes is mine!" said one of the young warriors with suppressed rage.

"Any Kumoku in front of me is a dead man," proclaimed another.

The elders continued with their lesson on battle attitude.

"Remember, numbers do not win battles, courage does. The war is only over when we have won and when the last man standing has gone down."

This brought from his memory stories he had heard about his tribe. Kande Kumugl unexpectedly came across a war party of ten men from one of the neighboring tribes. A skirmish ensued and Kande Kumugl alone fought them. It took some time before other men from Akenku joined in. By the time the number reached five, Kande Kumugl and his warriors chased the enemy back and out of their lands. This event alone sent shockwaves across the land and has been a high standard of warfare ever since.

"As long as one is fighting, keep fighting," said the elders.

"Porugl, you and four young warriors will maintain the high ground. Go to Bindekai," said Ormar who was now in charge of tactics. "No one must know you are there."

He wanted to be in the front line but did not argue. For one, the Akenku, under no circumstance undermine the wishes of an elder. The Akenku proudly displayed this attribute as their way of life. No other tribe mastered fully this trait. Being born ahead of others had this advantage.

When an Akenku elder said, "I saw the sun first," no one argued. This behavior set them apart from all the other surrounding tribes for generations. The elders often reminded the young warriors that the Akenku tribe attained greatness in Kondaland because of this.

Ormar and the elders split the warriors into two groups. He placed each man according to their strengths and divided them equally. Each group had a skillful bowman, a spearman, an axeman, and a shield man. Right behind them would be the old men of the tribe, known as the last line of defense. These old men would not follow the main party to the meeting place, but remain back near the entrance of the village. In the event that the enemy advanced towards the village, they would hold the line of shields on bended knees, never to retreat at all costs. The elder who gave Porugl his war headdress and five others joked amongst themselves and smoked tobacco. Old men who could not move would remain in the *yal yungu*.

One of the elders, looking cross the land, in a solemn voice chanted an old war cry and when he finished, Porugl and his band of warriors responded with such vigor enough to rattle the earth from its bones. Kondai glanced at the *yal yungu*. The last time she had heard such a thunderous uproar was during Kande Kumugl's last pig killing ceremony. The echo from the voices gave her an intense feeling of fear. It didn't seem like they were going to demand compensation from the Kumoku. They were going to war. She dreaded the thought, but it kept coming to her really strong. She looked at Maie and Maie looked at her. She hoped that all would be alright. But the dread became overpowering.

"You go on and whatever you do, don't sit down for anything. Our men are going to battle, so as long as they fight, we have to keep standing. I'll catch up to you," said Kondai.

"I thought this was a compensation demand," said Maie.

"I know, just be aware," she said and ran back to her house.

Maie joined the other womenfolk, and they waited for the warriors to come. They would stand from afar and watch.

"Akenku," shouted Ormar.

The warriors, both novice and seasoned, stood up with bows in their hands, their quiver full, axes slung in their belts, hands tight, legs ready, eyes on him, and victory in sight.

"Akenku," he shouted again and all the warriors drew closer.

And together they chanted the warrior's creed, repeatedly.

"Defend the land, protect your family, uphold your tribe!"

Porugl hadn't felt so high since the day he escaped Kerwanba's jaws. His heart pounded against his chest as if to break free from his body. Right now, no man was going to stop him. He was a force of nature. Porugl, together with the warriors, felt invincible.

The main party came down the road heading towards the meeting place. Just before they separated, he caught sight of his mother running towards them.

"Mother, what is it? You shouldn't be here."

"I know son, I came to give you this."

Kondai handed a long ragged brown feather to him. It was the feather his father Gamba had picked up after being left by the Kekemba the day when Kande Kumugl breathed his last. Porugl remembered the day so clearly. After all these seasons, his mother had kept the feather until now.

"Go, your ancestors watch over you," she said and gave Porugl the feather.

"Thank you, mother," he said and tied the feather into his war headdress.

They didn't hug. It was a bad omen. Porugl and the four young warriors hurried to the foot of Bindekai Peak. Kondai and Maie, with all the other womenfolk, trailed behind the main troupe of seasoned warriors to the meeting place.

Porugl knew the perfect spot where they would keep an eye on whatever happened below. As they passed the entrance to the family grave, he stopped and looked up to where his father, grandfather, and ancestors lay.

"Nina, be with me," he said.

Waine stopped at his side.

"Come on, we have to go."

The other boys reached the spot already and waited. A black snake slithered quickly across his path as he ran a few paces after Waine. It kept nagging in his mind. He stopped for a moment and then continued running. It's just a snake being startled by the noise from all the running that they did, he thought. Porugl's mind was all over the place, trying to figure out if the incident meant anything at all.

Ningir, Mange and Panduma felt relieved when Porugl and Waine arrived. They kept a keen eye on the group of people making their way to the meeting place.

"Hey look, the tribe is about to reach the meeting place," said Ningir.

"The Kumoku are moving," said Panduma.

The troupe of warriors who flanked the main crowd remained hidden. Just then, a bird chirped wildly.

"Shh," said Porugl and looked tensely around. The other boys held out their bows with arrows already in place. A moment of silence passed, then the bird started chirping again.

Porugl beckoned everybody to be quiet and to crouch low on the ground. Everyone held their breath. The quiet forest felt uneasy. He whispered to Waine and Ningir to go and check around. Porugl and the others gazed intently as the two disappeared into the bushes. The bird didn't chirp again. After a long while, the two boys returned.

"It's nothing. We checked all the way to the other side," said Waine.

"We have to—"

A woman's loud shrieking below cut through Porugl's voice. All of them gazed down and saw people running everywhere in different directions. Many more screams followed as men shouted at each other. A line of men and shields deployed towards the Akenku.

"This is an ambush," said Porugl. "They are coming for war."

Suddenly, more screams came from the direction of their village. Thick smoke began to rise. A single spiral of smoke rose higher, followed by another and then another. Soon, the whole sky filled with thick smoke. This caused confusion to Porugl and his tribesmen. They heard children squeal amidst the melee.

"They are in the village!" Panduma yelled.

"We have to go down and help them," said Mange, pointing to the intense activity happening at the meeting place.

"No, we have to go back and defend our village," said Waine.

"Porugl, we cannot leave them there," said Ningir, looking down below.

By that time, many more women wailed. The Kumoku line of men and shields advanced further.

"I agree with Waine. What is the first duty of an Akenku warrior?" asked Porugl.

"Defend the land!" they all responded.

"Let's go," said Porugl, and they ran across and down the mountain range back to their village.

While running furiously downhill, Porugl pulled three arrows out from his quiver and held it in place, aimed ahead and ready to launch. All the young warriors behind him did the same. They knew the tracks, ridges and overgrowth and they all moved precisely and in unison, avoiding the stumps and low-hanging branches.

As they got closer to the village, they saw women and young children running here and there. Children cried, looking for their mothers amidst the thick smoke that changed its direction as the wind changed.

"Check the last line of defense," shouted Porugl, as they ran closer.

Coming up the last dip before the main road, Porugl saw the enemy of ten warriors running towards the last line of defense. The old men split into two groups. Three in front and some distance away from the other three at the back. Their shields stood upright while already on bended knees.

"Hold on, we are coming," Porugl shouted across.

The old men didn't respond to Porugl or pay any attention to him. They stood their ground while the enemy made its way towards them. On one hand, they held their shields and the other with their axes, ready for the enemy.

"Come here, you cowards," screamed Porugl and increased his pace towards the advancing war party. But the war party closed in on the first line of defense.

"Waine, go to the second line and don't move," yelled Porugl, "Whatever happens, don't move!" Mange and Panduma followed Waine, while Ningir followed Porugl.

Ningir kept close to Porugl, only to see the enemy war party slash the first three shields with the old men down. Their bodies slumped to the ground at the impact of all the axes. Still in full flight, Porugl launched the three arrows all at once, with all his might. One of the arrows found its mark as one of the enemy warriors fell awkwardly to the ground. He launched another three again. The other warriors saw Porugl and Ningir approaching and quickly found refuge in the nearby shrubs. While some continued to advance to the next line of defense. Porugl and Ningir halted in their advance by a hail of arrows. The two found cover in a banana patch nearby.

"I'm going over. You keep them engaged," Porugl said to Ningir and went around the banana patch.

It was just as well that he moved because, one of the enemy warriors who had crept in secret towards the two and swung his axe. Porugl shifted and caught his hand and in one motion pulled an arrow out of his quiver, driving it into the man's eye. The man screamed and fell to the ground, holding the arrow still stuck in his eye and writhing in pain. Porugl plucked out one arrow from his quiver and shot the man. The arrow went into the other eye and all the way out the back of his head lodging itself in the ground.

Ningir kept the enemy warriors busy while he crouched around towards the back. After a short while, he saw a couple of warriors running frantically with Porugl hot on their heels. While running Porugl, got an arrow from his quiver, placed it on his bow and let loose the arrow all in one motion. The arrow found its mark going through the back and out the front of one warrior, forcing him to fall forward on his face. The others saw this and changed their direction towards the river.

Ningir came out of the banana patch, advancing to the remaining last line of defense. As he ran, he saw briefly the bodies of the three old men slain by the enemy. Lots of blood soaked the earth. He took his eyes away from the sight and continued. The other enemy warriors who had been engaging with Waine and his group saw what happened and fled. Waine, Panduma, and Mange followed Ningir and Porugl as they maintained their chase all the way to the river.

"What did I tell you? I said, don't move," Porugl berated Waine.

They all sprinted back to the remaining last line of defense. The three old men didn't change their stance.

"Have they gone?" they asked.

"Yes," said Porugl.

The old men stood and let go of their shields. The boys huddled around the old men and, hugging each other, they wept.

"Dewe Kumugl?" asked Porugl, referring to the old man who had given his war headdress.

Ningir looked at Porugl and shook his head, not wanting to tell him Dewe Kumugl was slashed across the face and neck.

"Nooooo," he cried, holding onto Waine for support.

"Go and bring our brothers back quickly," said one of the old men, holding back his tears.

"Our village is burning," said another.

Some of the women and children who hid among the nearby bushes came out cautiously. The young warriors brought them in and went to look for others.

"We will remain here. Our brothers have died gracefully and we want to follow them. You go and check the village. They need you," said the old men.

The young warriors brought back the bodies of old men in the first line of defense.

"Go now and leave us. We have to defend the land," said one of the old men with tears in his eyes.

Porugl and the young warriors got up and walked towards their village. The smoke filled their lungs and hurt their eyes. When the wind changed direction and cleared the smoke, Porugl and his brothers saw the destruction the enemy had left behind. They burned every Akenku house to the ground.

Just then, a group of warriors came out from the nearby bushes. All the young warriors in one action aimed their arrows in the direction of the noise.

"Stop, it's us," shouted Ormar.

"They ambushed us. We escaped with our lives, all our warriors, killed by the Kumoku."

"What about those near the river?" asked Porugl.

"We didn't hear any word from them. Round up all the women and children. Bring them to the foot of Bindekai.

That is where we will make our last stand," said Ormar. "They planned it all along. They wanted to wipe us out from Gandia. But they didn't do it alone, they had help."

Porugl wanted to know what really happened at the meeting place. Ormar shook his head and gazed into the distance.

"They seemed...different...somehow. We didn't talk after they saw us at the meeting place. They came from nowhere and attacked us. They had been waiting for us, too many and they overpowered us, they fought with a ferocity that we have not experienced and then..."

"And then what?" Porugl asked impatiently. "Keep an eye on the ridges," Porugl yelled as his brothers came closer.

"There was a..."

"A what? said Porugl.

"Giant...a huge monster of a man...he...he was so big and had one eye."

"And?"

"I...he was," Ormar was already teary.

"Ormar" Porugl said, nearly shouting at him.

Ormar shook his head. He was distraught, and his mind had not recovered from the ordeal. Porugl would ask later. They had to move up into the mountains before nightfall.

"We have to go. If they come back for a second wave, we won't be able to withstand them," insisted Waine.

Porugl left and went to check on the women and children. Maie and Kondai were amongst them.

"Waine, are we safe to move now?"

"Looks safe enough to go," said Waine.

Porugl came to Ormar and lifted him up.

"We have to leave."

Ormar hugged Porugl and led the villagers out under the watchful eyes of the remaining warriors. Women wanted to cry, but Ormar shut them. The sun had just crossed over the sky. Porugl and others kept watch as the women and children made their sad journey up to Bindekai. Exhaustion and depression reeked among them and most of all, they felt fear like never before. Some warriors remained in the bushes to keep an eye out.

Porugl came and sat by the fire with Ormar. Everyone contemplated what had just happened.

"We built temporary shelters against the rock face," said Ormar.

Porugl didn't say anything. Ormar knew he wanted to know more about this monster he had just seen.

"Irawam Toglkumba," said Ormar.

"Ehh?"

"That's his name, the one-eyed giant."

"Isn't that a bedtime story to scare small children into sleeping?"

"I saw him. He is as real as the Bindekai Mountains itself."

Porugl sat there thinking. He heard the story of Irawam Toglkumba, which means, Toglkumba, son of Ira, a one-eyed giant who lived with the *gigls* or spirits far north of the land.

A long time ago, a *gigl yagl* or male spirit found a woman from the Tambaiku tribe crying near the river one late afternoon. After many years of marriage, she didn't bear her husband any offspring and went to the river to commit suicide. The *gigl yagl* pitied her and visited her for many days. The woman bore a male child. But to her dismay, the child had only one eye and was ghastly looking. The woman couldn't bear to look at the child and took her own life. A lone hermit called Ira found the child crying amongst the marshes near the river. He named the child Toglkumba because his mouth split. Ira gladly took in Toglkumba. The male child didn't stop growing and grew into a huge and powerful creature. Many people who came across Toglkumba ran for their lives. Slowly, his story spread across the distant lands and the name Irawam Toglkumba stuck. He came out only during festive seasons, such as pig-killing ceremonies. People would stand and awe at his girth and height. But they never looked directly into his eyes. The huge single eye in the middle of his forehead saw everything. He had a huge appetite for meat and captured young girls.

"Their shields opened, and he came running at us," Ormar's voice broke Porugl's thoughts.

"We heard the loud thud of his footsteps coming at us. Our arrows did nothing to him. He smashed our shields and grabbed two of our men and went back. The men screamed as he tore their limbs apart and gulped it greedily while they were still alive. He didn't bother to kill them first."

This story shocked Porugl.

"Then he came again, blood still dripping from his wide ugly mouth. He grabbed another two from the defensive line our warriors held and went back again. Our arrows and spears did little to him, and while we focused on him, the Kumoku and Tambaiku advanced and killed many of our men. Toglkumba was hungrily feeding when we made our escape. I can still hear their screams in my head."

Porugl felt sick. He chose a spot near the fireplace and lay down. They had ordered the night watch. Ormar called to all the remaining warriors, which numbered less than a third, to gather around.

"The Kumoku will finish off what they started. They have now joined with Tambaiku, they ambushed us," explained Ormar. "They have been our tribal enemy for generations. For generations, they who suffered countless times. Now, they will savor their victory and finish us completely."

Gloomy faces made the dark night overbearing. The interesting enthusiasm and energy before the fight had disappeared. Their eyes said it all. With no pride and no will to build on, no strength and no hope, the Akenku remained quiet. What they thought would never happen, just happened and in an instant their lives overturned into an uncertain future.

"There are two options: we retreat and seek refuge in another land or we fight till the last man."

This would be the first time in the history of the Akenku tribe to go into *wandike* which means to seek refuge. The warriors gathered closer to the fire.

"They will not allow us to re-gather. They will strike while we are weak," said Ormar.

No one made an attempt to utter any words of encouragement. Porugl stared into nowhere. Life in Gandia would change forever.

~

All the realms in the Underworld heard what happened and remained aghast. Goglko, the *makan nem*, stood and watched in repulsion as the Kumoku secretly invaded the unprotected Akenku land, burning down all the houses. He felt like breaking his Underworld bond and wreaking havoc on this treachery. *Makan nem*, like Goglko, respected man's decisions and never took sides. All beings, both in the Outerworld and Underworld, upheld this understanding. But the action by the Kumoku incensed Goglko. He felt a heaviness inside and a deep sadness he didn't know existed came forth. Women and children went here and there, running away from the destruction as he stood helpless, knowing he couldn't get involved. He recalled an old Underworld saying, "When the balance of life is broken, there is only one outcome."

The two worlds didn't interfere with each other. If that balance broke, it could not be undone and both of the two worlds would descend into anarchy. And Goglko knew the outcome would be far more grievous than what was occurring around him at the moment. When the last structure crumbled into cinder, and the dust settled, Goglko returned. The tremors and echoes of the war above juddered through the walls of the Underworld. They gathered on the banks of the lake, looking out for him when Goglko arrived. Once out of the water, he did what he had never done in all his life. He stopped and addressed all the creatures, pipe still in his mouth.

"This is the treachery of man. Be careful underlings," he said in his high-pitched voice.

All the creatures returned to their abodes and dread what Kerwanba would do next. The minions skipped, danced, and pranced on their way to report the mayhem Toglkumba caused. Now, it all became clear to them why she didn't kill the halfling many seasons ago.

"Don't get too cocky. Porugl is not dead yet," she said.

"Ancient serpent. Soon, they will forget him," said Agandua.

"He is an imposter. The real Son of the Underworld is Irawam Toglkumba," she said. "Let the realms know, because of his insolence, I release Irawam Toglkumba."

The minions whispered this into the crevices and holes of all the realms, and they became aware. No creature in the Underworld remembered a time when Kerwanba called upon the Outerworld to do her bidding. She didn't bother herself with these thoughts. She had only one thing in her mind; Porugl's death. The seeds of destruction planted by her minions in Dengg's mind had found its mark.

When Porugl's realm heard Kerwanba calling him an imposter, they became agitated. Their joyous countenance and lively state had been severely affected when Gandia was completely destroyed and its warriors reduced to less than a third. They didn't know how to respond when they heard from Goglko the destruction that happened. They moved sullenly around in their realm. They had been waiting for the next occasion to get into Kerwanba's mind, and she had provided that opening herself.

They heard the vibrations coming in that Porugl was an imposter and Irawam Toglkumba was the real Son of the Underworld. The spark that nearly went out suddenly burned bright again. **Son of the Underworld** was the name they gave to Porugl. Kerwanba had no right to steal that title and give it to this monster. The time it took to congregate was faster than usual and the noise much louder.

Nondo and Milime came out of their abode and joined the group. They also heard the vibrations. Goglko stood at a distance and watched. When Kewand Kumugl wanted to say something to address the crowd, they shouted him down and called him a betrayer. They had seen him begging for his life in exchange for his services to Kerwanba. Some even tried to drown him in the lake and the two other humans had to save him. Goglko and Nondo, even Milime, didn't make any attempt to speak for Kewand Kumugl, who had already sold his services to the serpent.

"Son of the Underworld is a title this realm gave to Porugl and Kerwanba has no right to steal this title," said one creature.

"She has terrorized us forever. Now she is a thief," said another.

They began chanting 'thief, thief ,thief'.

"Quiet," said the first creature.

"You all will feel the pain of her venom," said Kewand Kumugl from his abode.

"Shut up," they all shouted.

Some of the creatures and beings rushed to him, but Goglko got in the way. "He is bound to Kerwanba. If you kill him, you will take up the place. Do you want to be in debt to Kerwanba?" asked Goglko.

"We know that she fears us. How? She has taken the name we gave to Porugl and has given it to this monster. She fears us. She fears Porugl," the creature shouted.

Nondo, Milime, Goglko and the three humans looked nervously around. Kerwanba would have heard the commotion already and would be on her way.

"The Outerworld betrayed him, the Underworld saved him," said one of the beings in the crowd, and kept repeating it.

The underlings, already emotional, responded and kept repeating with increasing intensity. 'The Outerworld betrayed him, the Underworld saved him, The Outerworld betrayed him, the Underworld saved him, The Outerworld betrayed him, the Underworld saved him'.

The creature who spoke watched helplessly as the tempo rose and rose, and the volume increased to decibels never experienced before until they blasted the rooftops of the cavern, 'Porugl Son of the Underworld'.

"Oh no, now we are really going to get it," said Nondo and he told Milime to go inside.

"Not if I block her entry," said Goglko.

"Are you able to do that?" asked Nondo. He had a frown on his face.

Nondo, as old as Kerwanba may seem, all of us were in the Outerland before the Kundawii. Even Mando, your leader, was there as well. Those of us who know the balance also know the deep, dark secret she holds. We just are not as power hungry as her."

"We are outsiders, they are natives, let Kerwanba deal with them," said Kewand Kumugl.

They didn't want to hear more and dispersed. Goglko went to the place where he and Porugl had shared a smoke many seasons ago and put up a crystal wall and returned to his realm.

Just as they expected, the underlings felt the cavern walls shake. Kerwanba was on the move. She bumped rock edges and corners, cutting herself. It didn't bother her. She came with rage to shut down the realm. She had never done anything like it in the history of the Underworld. It would be the first. The creatures and beings all scampered to the farthest edge of the cavern, away from the opening where she would come. They waited and heard the rumble, but she didn't appear. After a while, the underlings tired and some made their way back to their abodes.

Goglko had placed a crystal wall with a looping spell on the entrance. He knew Kerwanba would eventually know it was him. Kerwanba came to the crystal wall and returned to her starting point. After going around several times, she became exhausted and gave up.

"Minions," she screamed. "Go finds out who put that spell on the entrance."

9

Wandike

P orugl and his warriors drifted off into a deep sleep as exhaustion crept in. The touch of cold fingers woke Porugl abruptly. No sound came out of his mouth, though he tried to speak. A dark figure hovered over him. The figure was familiar to Porugl.

"Kewand Kumugl?"

The dark figure nodded and motioned Porugl to be quiet. The figure hovered away and beckoned Porugl to follow him. Dawn broke and Porugl saw the features of the old man he lived with in the Underworld.

"I come to you from the Underworld, a lot of things are happening and I come to warn you of grave danger," said Kewand Kumugl.

"You are late. Maybe you didn't see what happened to us today," said Porugl.

"And this will not stop. There is more atrocity to come. That is why I asked a favor from Milime to bring me here."

"Aren't you breaking the balance?"

"I am trying to maintain the balance, besides I am a human. This law doesn't apply to me."

"What of Milime and Nondo?"

"Kerwanba has already marked the both of them for death for healing you and the *gwika* leaf incident, so Milime gladly sent me here, Porugl, the *gwika* leaf is what keeps the Underworld together, it is the main ingredient to make *sperraro*, a fine dust that sparkles and is the medium of trade, without *sperraro*, the Underworld would disintegrate into chaos, and since you have the last leaf that was emitted by the gwika tree, Milime and Nondo are held accountable."

All trade in the Underworld used *sperraro* as a currency made by specialist dwarves. A tiny portion of the *gwika* leaf is crushed with special limestone crystals only found in the dwarf realm, into fine powder. The fine powder sparkles when heated and is a highly sought item. Medicine men in the Outerworld also purchase sperraro as it enhances any medical remedy or spell that is being evoked on patients.

Business in the Underworld came to a halt when Nondo got the *gwika* leaf. He didn't let the dwarf realm know that he had the leaf. They would have killed him and got the leaf. Even Kewand Kumugl did not know.

"Anyway, that's not the reason why I'm here. Kerwanba has broken her own tradition and is using Irawam Toglkumba. She is behind the Tambaiku and Kumoku. They want to kill you. If you want your tribe to survive, you must die for them. The only way to save your world is to kill Kerwanba. We will be with you."

"What of Dikamb?" asked Porugl.

"My son, Kerwanba, killed Dikamb right after you came. Her last wish was for you to avenge her and her son."

With those words, Kewand Kumugl disappeared into the shadows.

It was beginning to get clear and Porugl was wide awake. It was not a dream. Kewand Kumugl had risked his life to come up to the Outerworld and inform him and for that he was grateful. All the remaining warriors and young men were up standing or sitting around the fireplace. They looked lost and dull. None of the fanfare that riveted through their bloodstreams a day before the ambush could be seen. There was no trace of the high and mighty tribal name of the Akenku on their faces.

"We have to make a decision. If the Kumoku know we are here, they will launch another attack," said Ormar.

No one responded.

"I am still proposing that we go into wandike…the loss we have suffered is too great."

"What about our allies? What about Wakiku? Aren't they going to help us?" asked one of the warriors.

"Dingan's mother is a Wakiku woman. The Wakiku came and retrieved Dingan's body and buried him. I think that is why they are hesitant to come and help us," replied another warrior.

Porugl became tense at the mention of Dingan's name.

"All our brothers are dead, our fathers are dead all in one day. There has to be a reason why all this is happening," said one of the younger warriors. His eyes were teary as he finished speaking.

"We should fight till the last man standing," said another warrior.

All the warriors gazed at him.

"Are you baffling," replied another. "Can't you see what they have done?"

"Shut up, stop talking like a woman," the warrior responded angrily.

"No, you shut up. How many people have you lost? I lost my father; he was killed before my eyes—"

"Well, avenge him and stop crying."

Then, the two warriors launched themselves at each other but were stopped by their tribesmen.

'Enough, the both of you!" shouted Ormar. "The enemy is out there. I know what our tribe stands for, but we are in a unique situation now, so I ask you this, do you want to fight or go into wandike?"

"Life was good until you arrived," said Bauglo, one of the young warriors.

Porugl turned to see who spoke. The others became quiet.

"We are facing all of this because of you. If you hadn't killed Dingan, we wouldn't be here, if you had not returned from the Underworld, everything would be fine," he snarled.

The tension in the silence escalated quickly.

"Hey watch your tongue, boy, before I cut it off," said Ormar.

"That is why the spirits are angry. You should have stayed back in the Underworld. Why did you come?" said Bauglo.

He was stressing every word. Porugl didn't take his eyes off him. His grip on his axe grew.

"Are you supporting Dingan?" said Porugl, standing up.

All the warriors who were listening came in between quickly.

"This has nothing to do with what we are facing right now," said Ormar, trying to break the line of thought. "What happened to Dingan is an internal matter, and we have resolved ourselves."

"Porugl didn't start this, the Kumoku did," said one of the elders.

"How do you know?" asked another warrior.

"Enough!" said Waine.

The Akenku lost everything in one day. Houses burnt down, food crops and gardens destroyed, trees felled, animals slaughtered and many lives lost. The warriors struggled to comprehend why such a magnitude of destruction had happened in a brief span of time. They questioned themselves about what they had done as a tribe to bring such calamity up on themselves. In that emotional, mental state of mind, they accepted Baulgo's claim that Porugl caused this. They couldn't accept the fact that they had been defeated in the worst kind of way in all the history of the Akenku tribe.

"Hey there is someone coming," said one of the warriors.

"Get down everyone," said Ormar.

They all crouched. Porugl already drew his bow out, ready to release his hail of arrows.

Three warriors were hurrying up the slope towards them.

"It is I," called one of the approaching warriors and mentioned his name.

Everyone relaxed.

"The Kumoku were expecting us. They intercepted us before we could go to the primary group and help them. They came from everywhere. Many of our brothers lost their lives. We retreated to the river and hid until now," they reported.

"They are preparing to attack again. What are we going to do?" they asked.

"That's what we are discussing," said Ormar.

Discussions around the fireplace focused on what should happen next. Porugl sat by himself thinking about what Bauglo said. In a way, Bauglo was right. Hearing all the stories of the Underworld about Kerwanba, and then the visit by Kewand Kumugl confirmed that the ancient serpent had something to do with this. Porugl recalled the events leading up to him beheading Dingan. He knew very well the powers of Kerwanba. If the *gigl* can attack humans in the Outerworld, what more could she do? The more he considered it, the more it made sense. Upon this realisation, a feeling of great despair swept over his heart. If anything, Kewand Kumugl had confirmed that Kerwanba had a hand in all that happened. He made up his mind to bring the

Kumoku down. He would go into their lands and do the same, what they did to him and his tribe. He made up his mind that the Kumoku would feel the same pain he and his tribe felt.

Just then, a thought came so strong in his mind, 'You came to show us where we came from, you will show us where we are going'. His grandfather, Kande Kumugl, the great chief of Akenku, who on his deathbed had uttered these words and blessed him when he was in his seventh season.

Feeling much stronger, he got up. The talking subsided. The elders and Ormar who were deep in conversation, stopped. Porugl stood in the morning sun's glare.

"Many of you know the story of how one wrong turn led to many bad events. I cannot apologize for what happened already, but I will say this. I am here now and I will fight and die for the tribe."

The elders shook their heads and wanted to interject, but Porugl stopped them and continued speaking.

"I will go to Dawake and slaughter all the Kumoku, I will burn their houses down and do whatever it takes to restore and preserve our tribe. I ask that the Akenku tribe now go into wandike."

There was a finality about his voice that suppressed any thought of disagreement from Ormar or the elders. They recognized the presence of the great Kande Kumugl in him.

"Numbers do not win battles, courage does," he said.

"I will fight and die with you," said Waine in a loud voice, and stood up.

"My brother forever," replied Porugl.

Then Ningir, Panduma and Mange all stood up and voiced that they would join him. Panduma struggled to stand up. An arrow had grazed his ribs.

Porugl took a deep breath. A feeling of sadness enveloped him and he asked Panduma.

"Are you sure about this?"

"Porugl, I have as much right to avenge my family. You will not turn me away. I can still fight," said Panduma.

"I will be with him and assist him," said Bauglo.

The young warrior realized that what he said was going to lead to an action that would impact the tribe's existence forever. If he didn't follow Porugl, he and his household would be the brunt of scorn for generations to come. Even Waine, the funny guy, found the courage to go with Porugl. If he didn't make a move now, the tribe will jibe him and his family forever. They would accuse him of having no courage, and such accusations stuck around for many generations in tribal life. He had no choice but to follow Porugl and his band of warriors.

Ormar beckoned everyone to be quiet and called to the six young men.

"Come and stand before us."

The six young warriors, led by Porugl, moved to the front.

"We will now release you to do what you have to do," said Ormar.

He then instructed the other warriors to bring a pig and some banana leaves. Ormar and the elders slit the pig's throat and dripped its blood onto prepared banana leaves. Once the blood completed dripping, they wrapped the banana leaves and placed it over the embers of the fire. Ormar operated on the slain pig. All the limbs, backbone, and head were separated. The intestines were removed and offered to the spirits of the forest. Then Ormar told the warriors to come and cut the meat into pieces and roast it over the fire.

"By birth, you were born of many mothers. By death you will be united as brothers," he said and gave them the baked pig blood. They ate some of the roasted pork meat as well. "Go up to the ancestral grounds and eat this. When you return, we will not be here."

The warriors then gave their remaining quiver of arrows to the six young warriors. The womenfolk and children were stationed not far from where the men were. Maie was distraught, like everybody else. She went over again and again in her mind, if she deserved this. She had been a good girl all her life. She listened to her parents and conducted herself in a respectable manner.

"Maie, daughter here have something to eat," said Kondai and handed a sweet potato to her.

Maie broke away from her thoughts.

"Is Porugl there? Have you seen him?" asked Maie.

"Porugl is there, one of the women saw him. But don't go around asking. Many women have lost their husbands and sons. Just keep to yourself. The elders will tell us what to do. I know Kande Kumugl is watching with a sorrowful heart and I'm sure it will turn out all right."

She sighed. "I need to see him," said Maie.

"I know, and you will, but not right now," said Kondai.

The six warriors made their way up to the sacred burial ground. The place had both bad and good memories. Many seasons ago, Dingan tricked Gamba and pushed him off the cliff in this same spot. The Kekemba had saved Gamba.

The top of the peak revealed a spectacular view of the land. The bones of all Akenku lay strewn everywhere. A slight breeze blew and the young men took different spots and peered over the land. A lot of noise came across the river.

Porugl peered up the highest point of the peak, to Kekemba's nest. As a young boy, he enjoyed coming up here. The view gave him a sense of peace and belonging.

"Porugl," said Waine. "Let's eat while it is hot."

"Did you bring any sweet potatoes? I'm starving."

"Yes, but we will have them after."

Porugl joined the five boys, and they sat down to eat. Porugl opened the banana leaves, and the steam came out, revealing the freshly baked pig's blood. The aroma made them salivate because all of them had not eaten for a while now.

"I would not be able to do this alone. I thank you for giving your life to the tribe as I have," he said and cut the baked blood, giving each a portion. "Eat and rest. We move in the afternoon."

After seeing the boys off, Ormar addressed the rest of the warriors.

"Do not despair or feel depressed, they are doing what they can for the tribe, you are doing what you can for the tribe, we don't know how wandike will turn out, but the tribe needs to be protected, and that is now your responsibility."

Ormar went to the women and children. They stopped what they were doing and gathered around him.

"I don't know how to say this, but I will say it. We are going into wandike. We will seek refuge with the Wakiku tribe. Gather up what you have. We are leaving now."

With that, he called to the men.

"Have the boys watching over the village returned?

"Yes, they have," one replied.

"Take your positions, the first party in front, women and children in the middle, and the last party at the back. Move it," yelled Ormar.

"I don't see Porugl," said Maie shakily to Kondai.

"Wait, let me ask Ormar."

Kondai took quick steps to catch up to Ormar.

"I don't see Porugl. Where is he?" asked Kondai.

"Kondai," said Ormar and took a deep breath. He opened his mouth to speak but held back when Maie caught up to the both of them.

"Say what you have to say. She has every right to hear it," said Kondai.

Ormar shook his head. "He won't be joining us, he chose to take a different path."

"What path?" said Maie.

"He has chosen to make war with the Kumoku, I…I'm sorry, but I have to lookout for the tribe. Please understand, everyone has lost something in this fight," he said and continued walking. "I tried to talk to him, but he is just like his grandfather. Once he says something, that's it, he won't change his mind."

Maie and Kondai stood there, holding each other. Maie was sobbing.

"Why, mother why," cried Maie.

Kondai held Maie's hand and soothed her.

"Daughter, I don't know why. We will see."

"What about his child I am with, Porugl, oh Porugl," lamented Maie.

"Oh, my poor daughter, did you tell him?"

Maie shook her head. "I was about to tell him, then…" Maie didn't complete her sentence.

"Keep those women down," shouted one of the warriors.

A few of the women came and comforted Maie and Kondai.

"We have to keep moving," said one of them.

10

Irawam Toglkumba

Across the river, the Kumoku celebrated their greatest victory against the Akenku. They slaughtered many pigs and brought the choicest foods. Every household accommodated the visiting tribe from the north. Surrounding tribes also witnessed the victory celebrations. A big *ambai kango* or courting session took place. Tambaiku warriors courted young girls from the Kumoku openly. Even some married women took part in the courting to the distaste of their husbands. Dee Kumugl, chief of the Kumoku, didn't say anything. This victory established him and put to rest any doubts and misconceptions about his leadership. Never would anybody say anything negative to him or his family. Bindi Kumugl, chief of the Tambaiku, took center stage as the real hero of the battle. He enjoyed all the attention and focus with his newlywed bride. Where Bindi Kumugl went, Dengg followed. Tambaiku warriors received the choicest pork as leaders gave pompous speeches.

"Eat and enjoy, warriors of Tambaiku and women of Kumoku, as I have married into the tribe, so must all your daughters be our brides."

The crowd roared its approval.

"Maybe one day, all the warriors of Kumoku will come to Mondaugl and court all our daughters."

A greater roar of approval ensued.

"Men and women of the great Kumoku tribe, now for the surprise you all waited for...I give you Irawam Toglkumba, the real Son of the Underworld."

The minions rejoiced as Bindi Kumugl mouthed the words they had planted in his head.

At this, all the Tambaiku warriors got together and roared a thunderous roar and led the man-monster into the village. Many had not seen him yet, and many more didn't know such a creature existed. They had heard myths about this half-man, half-beast. The Tambaiku brought him secretly and unleased him into battle. Stories came back to the Kumoku that a giant destroyed the Akenku. Amidst the celebrations, most of the talk focused on Irawam Toglkumba. They all wanted to see him and pleaded with Dengg to tell her husband.

The villagers scurried to get a glimpse of the giant being led into the village. Men, women, and children clamored at the entrance in a flurry of movement to see the monster. Dancers, mostly men, beat their drums and the escorting party rushed out before him in mock battle stance, called *kai-gagle*. Kumoku warriors roared the traditional welcome.

Toglkumba moved to the beat of the drums with the Tambaiku warriors. The tallest warrior barely reached his breasts. Children clung to their mothers and hid their faces. His huge stomach protruded out before him, shaking with every step. He had no hair on his body and head. No one dared to look directly at his one-eye located in the middle of his forehead. There was a ghastly scar on his upper lip and two holes below his eye formed his nose. He had no teeth in the front part of his upper gum. Toglkumba had no earlobes, just holes in the side of his head. The crowd moved along as he kept moving.

Children paid no attention to their parents who told them to stop staring at his eye. They rushed to keep pace with him, bumping into each other along the way. Just then, he leaned down, opened his enormous eye, and poked his tongue through the gaping hole in his gums. Children screamed in fright and in delight. Others stumbled to get away. Men and women berated their children. The drums kept beating, and he kept bouncing along. The entourage reached the end of the village, and the drums stopped. The warriors stopped everyone from following. They brought Irawam Toglkumba to his temporary abode and heaped lots of pork and food for him while warriors stood watch.

The celebrations and shouting receded, but men still courted women. Those that found agreement left secretly and went in different directions. Bindi Kumugl signaled Dee Kumugl and the elders of the Kumoku to him.

"I want to be with my bride, but we have to discuss a few things first."

"Come, let us go into the *yal yungu*," said Dee Kumugl and led them.

Once inside, Bindi Kumugl called on Dengg to join them in the *yal yungu*. This move caught the seasoned warriors and the elders by surprise. In all their knowledge, no woman had ever entered the *yal yungu*. But no one dared to mention it.

"Dee Kumugl, any reports from the scouts that you sent?" asked Bindi Kumugl.

"Yes, the Akenku village is totally destroyed. No life, tree or animal remains."

"Good and what of this, Porugl?"

"Porugl?" asked Dee Kumugl

"Yes, Porugl," replied Bindi Kumugl, looking directly at Dee Kumugl and incensed that he answered with another question.

Dee Kumugl didn't want to show that he had not thought about checking specifically for Porugl.

"He is dead, his head is on a spit," said Dee Kumugl.

The Kumoku warriors glanced at each other, knowing their chief lied about Porugl. None of them had checked if indeed Porugl was dead.

"Well, that is good. Launch a search and destroy party to the Akenku land tomorrow. They should cover the length and breadth of Gandia to make sure the land is free. Kill any remaining survivors. I want to settle the Tambaiku in the new lands with my young bride. I will leave now with my bride, we have much to do," he said and touched his bride's thigh.

Commotion burst in the *yal yungu* after Bindi Kumugl and his Tambaiku warriors left. Dee Kumugl watched Dengg and the old chief leave and thought about them.

"There are so many things wrong here," said one of the elders. "The Akenku don't believe in numbers, they believe in courage, we will still face them."

"We have already brought the destruction to ourselves. This woman should have never entered the *yal yungu*. It is a bad sign right in front of us. Now calamity will come," said another elder.

"Stop it," said Dee Kumugl with a strong voice. "I know what I saw. Our main concern now is to know if Porugl is truly dead."

"My chief, you should have told Bindi Kumugl the truth," said one of the warriors.

"And make ourselves look stupid. You should have used your head and checked," said Dee Kumugl

"Who knows what the boy looks like?" said the warrior.

"He spent most of his life in a hole. We don't know what he looks like and we don't care," said another warrior

They all agreed to maintain Dee Kumugl's story.

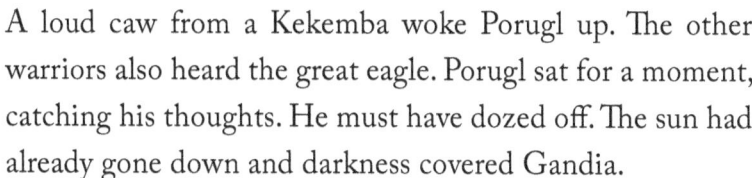

A loud caw from a Kekemba woke Porugl up. The other warriors also heard the great eagle. Porugl sat for a moment, catching his thoughts. He must have dozed off. The sun had already gone down and darkness covered Gandia.

"We need to go," said Porugl and rose. The others followed him as he led the way down.

A tomb-like silence devoured the grim scene before them. No bird or evening crickets chirped. Man and nature, it seemed, had left this land. Porugl felt a pang of pain in him as he and his band of warrior brothers walked through the place where once houses stood.

"Hold it," someone whispered from the back.

Every one froze.

Porugl turned around. "What is it?" he said.

"Look," said Ningir and pointed across.

As they came closer, all of them got a shock at their lives seeing the severed heads of their tribesmen on sticks. Their mouths opened terribly. Some had their eyes closed, while others still had their eyes open. Insect and flies swarmed around the heads, moving in and out of the ears, nose, and mouth. Some had maggots falling out of their necks onto the ground. The young warriors became aware of the increasing stench as they drew near. A couple of dogs who had taken down one of the severed heads scampered away at the approach of the warriors. Waine lifted his bow and scanned the area.

Porugl shivered at the scene and stood there transfixed. His stomach churned and threatened to spill out the baked pig blood.

"What shall we do?" asked Ningir.

It was getting darker and creepier by the moment.

"Let's make a big fire. Get all the remaining wood you can find," said Porugl.

The boys quietly went and searched for remains of wood from the houses that were burnt.

"You keep watch," he said to Panduma.

One by one, the boys brought wood in and arranged it to form a platform.

"Don't look at them, say sorry and pick the heads up by the stick, and lay them on the platform. We cannot give them a proper burial, but this is the best we can do," said Porugl.

The boys didn't fully understand what he said and hesitated. Porugl went and stood in front of the head nearest to him, said sorry, and pulled out the stick with the head still attached. He brought the head back and placed it on the platform. The boys did the same and after a while; they piled all the heads on the platform of wood.

"Thank you for defending the land. Come with us, we are going to the Kumoku," he said and set alight the wooden platform.

Tears rolled down all their faces. The wind blew and set a big flame on the platform as the young warriors left and crossed the river into Kumoku territory.

Someone in the Kumoku village who was relieving himself saw the brightly lit fire across the river. He came hurriedly into the village and announced for all to see. People came out of their houses from their sleep or whatever business they were doing. Dengg and Bindi Kumugl also went out and saw the fire.

"See, what did I tell you? Some of the Akenku are still there," said Bindi Kumugl.

"You are wise, my chief," said Dengg. "Will Toglkumba go tomorrow with the war party?"

"No, my lovely wife."

"Tell the war party to bring Porugl's head back."

"Ahhh, very smart of you, my lovely wife."

Dengg had been planning how she would leave the old chief. But she had to be sure of Porugl's death before she absconded. She needed Bindi Kumugl to be focused on killing Porugl. From the conversation she heard in the *yal yungu* earlier that day, she knew the warriors had not killed Porugl. For now, she kept Bindi Kumugl satisfied emotionally and physically.

"We will come in the morning. Wait for us there," shouted one of the warriors across the river.

A thunderous roar of approval followed.

"I hope you liked your gifts on the sticks," said another warrior.

Another roar followed with laughter.

Further up along the ranges that formed the Bindekai Peaks, the remaining Akenku tribe rested. The journey dragged on with women and children. Ormar found a spot they would regain their energy. The fire below caught their attention. Some of the women were weeping when they saw the light.

"That's Porugl and his warriors," said Ormar, wiping the tears coming from his eyes.

"They are letting us know where they are," added one of the women.

"We are with you son, we are with you and all your brave warriors. May the spirit of your ancestors bring you back as they brought your father back from the peaks of Bindekai," said an old woman.

'Kande Kumugl, you brought him to me from the depths of the earth, and I know it is not for him to die like this,' Kondai thought.

"Maie, come my child, Porugl fights for us," she said as she held Maie.

The Akenku continued on their journey the next day with only the front party. The rear guard left during the night and headed to the river at a different location. Early in the morning the next day they shouted their war cry three times and waited. After a while, a loud roar came from across the river. The Tambaiku and Kumoku hurled insults and demeaning words at the Akenku.

'How did the heads of your bothers taste? We are coming to give you more. Wait for us," they shouted.

"They are still there, launch the attack," said Bindi Kumugl.

A horde of warriors crossed the river. The Akenku war party shouted one more time and retreated back up into the mountains. The Tambaiku and Kumoku advance party ran to the place, only to find it empty. All of them were on high alert.

"The land is empty," reported the scouts.

"This is a trick," said one of the warriors. "They will slay us. Let us go back."

"Stay where you are," said Goimbu in a booming voice.

Tambaiku's battle hardened commander glanced around. His own men feared him and stood still. The Kumoku heard stories about him. Rumours spread widely of him being a *kumo kwimbo* or that he possessed an evil spirit.

"You will do as you are told. Search all the Akenku lands…now!" he bellowed.

The war party broke into three factions and spread. They searched every ditch, bush, forest, river bank and cave. They found no one. The sun made its way from its mid-point by the time the searching war party had finished. One of the factions, with fewer warriors, returned earlier to the banks of the river.

"Let's wait for the others," said one warrior.

Others didn't bother and dived into the cool river.

"There is no one here. Let's go ahead, I'm hungry," said another and crossed the river.

He took the first step onto the banks when something struck his head and he fell backward into the river. The gushing river concealed the splash his body made. The arrow lodge firmly in the man's skull. Water beside the body turned red, and the current swept the body downstream.

One of the warriors on the other side noticed the motionless body going down with the current. Before he yelled a warning, two arrows clung to his body. One to his neck and the other to his chest. The others saw the arrows strike him and, in a state of confusion, crossed the river, but arrows took them down. The last warrior who had not crossed the river yet shouted and dashed back into Akenku land. Porugl put him in his sights and released one arrow to fly right after him. The arrow caught him in his back, going right through until the tip of the arrow protruded out of his stomach. He fell forward to the ground. Porugl and his warriors came out of their hiding places and finished off the remaining warriors, pushing the dead into the river and letting the current do the rest. The two factions heard the shouting and ran to the scene. Porugl saw a bigger group return.

"Mange, Bauglo and Ningir, go round and attack them from the back as we planned. But wait for the signal."

'What signal?" asked Mange

"You will know, whatever you do, don't retreat and focus on the front. Our lives depend on it. We will meet in the middle."

The three young warriors crept into the river further up and went around to the back of the returning Kumoku and Tambaiku war party.

'Where are the others?" asked Goimbu

"They must have gone ahead," said someone in the war party.

Thirsty and hot, they stooped down to drink water and cool themselves.

"There's blood here," said one warrior.

They all congregated to the pool of blood when a hail of deadly *yer arai* or assault arrows plunged down from the sky. The arrows clung onto the resting warriors. Warriors fell down dead, while others clutched the arrows stuck in their bodies and screamed in pain.

"They are attacking," cried Goimbu, "form the lines."

Some warriors didn't know what to do and retreated back into Akenku land. A hail of arrows from Mange, Bauglo and Ningir greeted them. A couple of warriors gathered but didn't see where the arrows were coming from. All three didn't launch their arrows at once. When Mange and Ningir launched theirs, Bauglo held back. And when Mange and Ningir were reloading, Bauglo unleased his. In that way, a steady stream of arrows kept coming at Kumoku and Tambaiku. The arrows spread as they got closer to the enemy and a lot of enemy warriors were falling down. While their attention turned to the Akenku land, Porugl, Panduma and Waine picked out the warriors one by one from the back. Confusion gripped the Tambaiku and Kumoku warriors. Arrows were coming from the sky, from the back and from the front. Some of the warriors fled downstream when they realized all of them would be killed if they stayed.

"Come back here, you cowards!" screamed Goimbu.

Bodies of Tambaiku and Kumoku lay everywhere. Some were motionless, others struggling to move to the river. At the end of it, Goimbu stood alone, with an arrow stuck in his thigh. He had his bow and arrow pointed towards the Akenku land focusing on the three warriors in front of him. Someone crossed the river, and he turned around. He didn't recognize the face. A young muscular man accompanied by two warriors checked all the bodies lying around and hacked to death those who were still breathing. They paid no attention to him. Goimbu let out a cry and released his arrow, but the arrow went astray as three arrows piled into his body before he let go of the bowstring.

Above, the Kumoku and remaining Tambaiku heard the commotion below.

"It could be a trap," said Dee Kumugl

'It is a trap. You are just as stupid as your father," said Bindi Kumugl.

"Send the other warriors with Toglkumba," said Dee Kumugl.

"You see, that's what I mean, stupidity runs in your bloodlines, let them have this day, send your men, the Kumoku to scout and find out what happened." Bindi Kumugl walked back into his hut and barked at Dengg to follow him.

The scouts returned from their mission later that evening. Dee Kumugl kept his distance from Bindi Kumugl, not knowing how he would react after hearing the report. They called him.

"What is it?" he said.

"It's not good," said one of the scouts, shaking his head.

"Tell me."

"They came from all over. Some of the men escaped to tell us the story. They are hiding at a nearby cave and scared to come in. They are afraid of you. They said the sky rained arrows. Arrows were flying from all over the land. From the top, from the back and the front.

"What?" Bindi Kumugl yelled and came closer to the scout.

"Where is Goimbu," he asked.

There was a moment of silence.

Where is Goimbu?" he yelled.

The atmosphere became tense. Tambaiku warriors looked around at the Kumoku. One of the scouts came forward slowly from behind and gave him Goimbu's head, which was still attached to the stick.

"Aiyaahhh!" cried Bindi Kumugl in a loud voice and fell down to the ground, still holding the spit and wailed intensely.

Men gathered and chased women and children away. The people talked in murmurs as Bindi Kumugl lay on the ground, still weeping.

"Into the *yal yungu*," said Dee Kumugl.

The warriors' countenance changed drastically in an instant. Goimbu, the most feared warrior of the far North, had been decapitated on a simple mission to eliminate the remnants of the Akenku tribe and establish Bindi Kumugl's claim over the Akenku land. He wanted all the glory to himself and insisted Goimbu lead the 'search and destroy' party. Right now, he felt lightheaded. His confidence diminished in moments.

Their past victories resulted because of Goimbus actioning Bindi Kumugl's plans and strategies with near perfection. Bindi Kumugl trusted no one else to carry out his wishes. Now with Goimbu dead, a great void in his life emerged. He felt empty, devoid of any pride, and sat alone without Dengg. The *yal yungu* was filled to capacity. Those who couldn't find spaces in the *yal yungu* stood around the entrance. The Tambaiku and Kumoku didn't expect to be in this situation.

"And who are the warriors who came back?" asked Bindi Kumugl.

"Only a few," replied the scout.

"Well, tell us what you saw," said Bindi Kumugl, getting annoyed.

Warriors interrupted the scout before he got past the first sentence. They pushed him to the front and yelled at him to speak louder. Looking nervously at Bindi Kumugl, he related what he and the other scouts encountered.

The mist had not cleared yet when they arrived very early in the morning near the river. They saw bodies of the slain all over the banks on both sides of the river. Some were on the ground face up, others lay face down, and a couple were on rocks in the river. All of them had more than one arrow pierced into them. The scouts freaked out and paused. They argued whether to proceed or to return. Finally, they crossed. More bloodied bodies lay inland. They continued cautiously and studied their surroundings. A twig crackled suddenly, and the scouts jumped in fright. They got close to each shaking. Someone appeared through the mist. They saw more of them emerging out of the mist with arrows pointed at them. The tall and muscular young man in the middle had an air of authority about him. One of the scouts peed and wet the feet of another scout. The man in the center spoke.

"You severed the heads of all my fathers and brothers, I have severed only one, go tell your people, I am not finished yet, there are two more heads I will severe," and he threw down Goimbu's head in front of the scouts.

The scouts fell back.

"Before you run back home, collect all the arrows and give them to us. Tonight, we will let you come and collect the bodies. We are the Akenku. We are not treacherous like you," said the young man.

"You what?" said Bindi Kumugl.

He stood and raised his axe at the scout.

"My chief," said the scout quickly and cowered down, "We left them and came. They collected arrows themselves."

The scout lied. He and the other scouts collected all the arrows and gave them to Porugl and his warriors. But if he said he collected the arrows, they would kill him instantly. The other scouts also followed suit to say that they left them and came.

"How many of them?" asked Bindi Kumugl.

"I…uh…I don't know…I couldn't see well, the mist—"

"How many!" yelled Bindi Kumugl.

"I saw three or four, I think," replied the scout timidly and asked his other colleague scouts, "How many did you see?"

"Four or five," replied one of the other scouts.

"There were many," called another scout hurriedly.

"We ambushed them. Now they are ambushing us," said one of the elders.

"Only a few appeared," said the first scout.

Bindi Kumugl glared at him in disgust.

The murmur between the men rose after listening to the scouts. Dee Kumugl had not spoken yet for fear of being derided in front of his tribe. The feeling of insecurity which had disappeared for a day came rushing back to him again. The confidence he wore like a badge after the Kumoku ambushed the Akenku was nowhere to be seen on his face. Amongst the murmuring, Dee Kumugl heard the men saying that Dengg coming into the *yal yungu* caused all of this mayhem. Others stated that the battle with the Akenku should have happened out in the open. Ambushing the Akenku for no reason at all had turned the spirits against them.

"Who is this man who talked to you?" asked Bindi Kumugl

All the murmurs died down quickly.

"I don't know," said the first scout.

"He said he would take two more heads," said one of the other scouts from the back.

"Obviously, it wasn't your head he was talking about," replied Bindi Kumugl.

The men didn't know whether to laugh or not. Dee Kumugl and the Kumoku already figured out the identity of the tall, muscular young warrior.

"They will pick us apart until we are no more. Whatever you want to do, Dee Kumugl, do it now," said another elder.

"What is your advice on this?" said Dee Kumugl.

The shocked elder glared at Dee Kumugl for putting him on the spot. In such contentious times, the chief confided with the elders in private and then made known his decisions in public. This unexpected question from Dee Kumugl in public angered the elder. Well, if he wants to know what I really think, I'll tell him, thought the elder.

"You attacked the Akenku for no reason at all, other than war. The spirits are on their side. This is no ordinary tribe. This is the Akenku we are talking about. My advice is to call out to the Akenku and tell them that both sides have lost many lives and that the fight is over."

Bindi Kumugl came on Dee Kumugl's invitation and sweetened the effort by offering Dengg's hand in marriage. Bindi Kumugl suffered a huge loss to his manpower. Bindi Kumugl would not accept anything else except war. He had to say what Bindi Kumugl wanted to hear. He might make an attempt to take his life if he didn't respond properly.

"My brothers from Tambaiku, my people from Kumoku, this is the Akenku we are talking about, yes I know and we slaughtered them. Our elder here is still living in his fear of the Akenku, but I am not. We would be stupid to think that they would just leave without retaliating. And it is our business now to finish what we started. Our losses have united us. We are now brothers. I will lead the advance party. We will finish whoever is still in Gandia tomorrow."

"Mangra!" shouted one of the warriors, and the *yal yungu* burst with the roar of the men.

"I'll be standing with you," announced Bindi Kumugl. "I will unleash Irawam Toglkumba."

The *yal yungu* roared again. After that, men talked confidently and shared tobacco. Some left to go and retrieve the bodies down at the river, while others stood watching for the Akenku. No one would go to their wives tonight. They would all spend it in the *yal yungu*. Bindi Kumugl knew he had to stay with the men in the *yal yungu*, but decided to spend the night with Dengg.

"That man, the one whom the scouts talked about, that is Porugl, I know it. He is still alive. No one could have done such a daring—"

"Shut up!" yelled Bindi Kumugl and slapped her.

Dengg yelped and cowered in the corner. She could taste blood in her mouth.

Bindi Kumugl stormed out of the hut. What was he thinking, he thought. Warriors never slept with their wives on the eve of battle. He felt disgusted at himself and went to check on Irawam Toglkumba.

II

Bogl the Wakiku Village

Standing on the edge of the Bindekai range, Ormar shouted in a loud voice across to the lands of the Wakiku, telling them that they, the Akenku, were coming to them. And that they, the Akenku, were seeking refuge or *wandike*, with them. He called his name, saying that it was he who was speaking.

The Wakiku were going about their normal village life when they heard Ormar's voice.

"We saw their village burning," said one of the Wakiku women.

"The fight might come to our village if we take them in," said one of the men.

"They are in wandike now, we will accommodate them," said Chief Anga of the Wakiku.

Chief Anga had roots in Akenku and reason to welcome the Akenku to their village. Chief Anga owed his life to Kande Kumugl. He had been courting a girl from the Kumoku during his young days. A dispute arose and Kumoku warriors chased Anga out of Dawake village. He tripped while running from the river into Akenku land. The Kumoku advanced and then fled the scene when they caught sight of Kande Kumugl. He told the young Anga to be on his way and not to tell anyone about the incident. Anga related the story when he and his tribe attended Kande Kumugl's funeral.

Anga Kumugl sent a war party to secure the incoming Akenku tribe and bring them into the village. By the time they arrived in Bogl, the Wakiku village, all the people gathered to see the Akenku tribe coming in. Some of the Wakiku had family in Akenku and when they saw them, rushed to greet them. The war party took the Akenku to the front of the *yal yungu*, where Chief Anga waited with a group of elders and warriors.

"I have heard of your plight and I am sorry. We don't know if the Tambaiku and Kumoku will stop at the Akenku lands. But for now, you are safe. We are grateful that you have chosen us to come into wandike."

Anga said that because he never returned the favor to Kande Kumugl. Even if he did try, Kande Kumugl would have bluntly refused him. Anga had another opportunity to return the favor when he contemplated joining Akenku in the battle. But he faced stiff resistance from Dingan's uncle. Dingan's mother came from the Wakiku tribe and her brothers had come down to Gandia and retrieved Dingan's body and buried him. They had expressed their anger and frustration, even demanding compensation before returning to Bogl. The Akenku had not got around to discussing it yet when the war erupted. When chief Anga and his elders talked about it, Dingan's uncles became very aggressive and threatened all sorts of things. Anga Kumugl felt sorry for the Akenku when he could not get involved. When the Akenku announced their *wandike* into Bogl, he gladly received them. He had waited a long time to show his gratitude to the Akenku, and the opportunity presented itself.

"Thank you uncle Anga Kumugl, chief of Wakiku," said Ormar in response. "The Kumoku ambushed us. We didn't know the Tambaiku formed an alliance with the Kumoku. They burnt everything down to the ground. Nothing stands. We will remember what you have done for generations. The woman that bore you is from Akenku and we are grateful. You and your tribe will be blessed by the spirits. From now on, I declare we shall be known as Akenku Wakiku."

A nod of approval came from all the elders and people gathered.

"All Wakiku, take one family each, share your gardens, keep the prime lands for yourself, lend the waste lands to them," said one of the elders.

Immediately, people moved about. The Wakiku went and selected each of the Akenku. They hugged and brought them home.

"Hey, you look like Maie," said a woman who was approaching Maie and Kondai.

"Yes," said Maie, unsure of who spoke to her.

"It's me—"

"Druwagle," exclaimed Maie. "What are you doing here?"

"What? How could you not have heard? I'm married here."

Druwagle had married into Kumoku previously, but her husband died. The husband's family kept their child, a daughter, and released her. Damba, a man from Wakiku, showed interest in her and they married. Damba's wife had also died.

"This is my mother, Kondai," said Maie proudly.

"Aiyeeh, I heard about your story, the rock lady of Gandia," said Druwagle.

Damba came and greeted the two women, and they chatted while walking back to where they lived. The small hut had no separation for sleeping. They apologized and Damba said he would build a bigger hut when Druwagle had children. Druwagle scoffed at him and went about preparing a meal, while Damba went out. Maie and Kondai rested as the journey uphill had been tiring.

Voices brought Maie out of her sleep. In the dim light of the fireplace, she saw Druwagle serving food. The aroma made her hungry. She and Kondai had not eaten properly for several days. Damba cut the tree chicken or "*ende konduagle*" into pieces and laid them on the leaves which had banana and vegetables. Maie excused herself and went out.

'If you want to relieve yourself, go to the other side," said Druwagle.

Maie stood outside. The cooler air made her shiver. Forest birds shrieked in the distance. The stars came out, and she wondered if Porugl saw the same stars. She caressed the bump on her stomach. Kondai had already awoken and eating when Maie came in.

"Here is your food," said Druwagle, and handed her a banana leaf with food.

Maie ate and listened to the two women talk. After the meal, Damba left for the *yal yungu*.

"Maie, your mother Kondai has told me I'm happy for you," said Druwagle.

"Thank you, but I don't know now. This child is going to be a bastard without a father," she said and quickly wiped her the tears. Her hands shook as she picked up a piece of banana.

"Maie, your husband is special. We, the Wakiku, have all heard the story about him. He carries with him his name and legacy, which is a burden on him. That is why he must do what he is doing now."

"I know," said Maie, still struggling to contain herself.

"I still believed Porugl would come back from the Underworld, even when everyone thought he was dead. This thought kept me alive and sane. Now, you have to be strong for him. Be strong and he will come back to you and your child," said Kondai.

Maie indicated that she wanted to sleep and dozed off after hearing the chatter of the two women into the night.

Men came to the *yal yungu* when Damba arrived. It would have been a quiet and ordinary night, but tonight, the din from the *yal yungu* rose higher. The arrival of the Akenku created a stir to the routine they lived. Damba saw Dingan's uncle studying him as he came in. He still resented the Akenku coming to Bogl. He would have to inform Anga about it. Anga and the elders talked amongst themselves, so Damba could not disturb him. One of the elders got everyone's attention.

"Tomorrow, you will share a small portion of your land with the Akenku. You are not giving them the land, you are sharing it. The Akenku will not own the land."

The elders then told the Wakiku how to treat and accommodate the Akenku. Working the land would keep their minds off the trauma of battle. The elders also warned the men of Wakiku not to take advantage of the Akenku women folk. There would be no courting of young girls and widows.

"The Akenku are now our family. We treat them like brothers and sisters," said Anga Kumugl.

"We will not entertain any thought. The men of Akenku need to build their own houses. Share your land to them," said another elder.

"I want all the young warriors of Wakiku to guard the Kakam range. Keep an eye out for what is happening down below. We will maintain this watch as long as the Akenku is here," said Anga.

The talks concluded, and Damba came to Anga.

"I still don't feel good about Dingan's uncle," said Damba.

"Yes, I know, but he cannot do anything," said Anga

"Do you think he will do something?"

"No, but if he does, then we will have to deal with him."

"Porugl's wife is pregnant."

"Alright, keep an eye out for her," said Anga.

Dingan's uncle watched the two men talking and went out of the *yal yungu*.

Sometime before mid-day the next day, Ormar came with Damba carrying freshly split wood and they piled it near the house. Druwagle heard the wood being dropped to the ground and came out of the house. The two men had left already, but she could see other men coming towards their house carrying wood. Kondai and Maie came out of the hut to see a large pile of wood in front of the house.

"What's happening?' asked Kondai.

"I think we are building a new house," said Druwagle

"Oh alright," said Kondai, already feeling guilty.

Damba needed privacy with Druwagle once in a while, but that couldn't be the case now, thought Kondai. As long as she and Maie stayed with them, the intimacy between Druwagle and Damba would be impossible. Thinking about it, she realized her body had completely forgotten what it felt like to be with a man? Ormar seemed a decent guy, but all that had to wait. She cursed herself for even thinking such thoughts.

Ormar took it on himself to build a house for Kondai and Maie. All the men had planned to fell a number of trees in the morning so the Akenku men could start building their houses. They started with Ormar and would proceed to help the others. This greatly reduced the workload and shortened the time.

"Maie, come, let's cook some food for these men. They will be hungry."

Just as Druwagle said, the men hauled in the next load of wood. Ormar and Damba came and, after adding wood to the pile, they sat down. Kondai eyed Ormar with suspicion and walked into the hut.

"It is crowded here, so we are building a new one for Kondai and Maie," said Damba.

Kondai heard what Damba said, confirming her thoughts about Ormar. She knew it the moment she saw him and she felt embarrassed.

"You need to make a big house for Kondai, not like the small one we have," said Druwagle.

"I will make a big house if there is a promise of children. I don't want to make a big house for nothing," said Damba, and laughed.

Kondai cringed inside the house. I will have a word with Ormar in private and tell him I am not interested, she thought.

"Maie, you and your mother will not remain with me like this. You need a man around the house. All of you are adults. I don't need to explain," said Damba.

"Sorry, Porugl is coming back. I'm fine," said Maie quickly.

"Hehe, yes Maie, I know, I'm talking about her," he said, indicating with his head in Kondai's direction.

Men came in carrying more wood.

"Come, come and let's serve the food," said Druwagle.

Kondai didn't come out of the house. She stayed inside until all the men had left.

"Come out, they have left," said Druwagle. "Come and have some food."

12

Retaliation

The young warriors heard the Kumoku uproar from the other side of the river. They ignored the blisters on their hands and aching arms and kept their mind on the plan that Porugl laid out. Panduma, the injured warrior, stayed close to Porugl. His condition didn't get any better. The young warriors didn't know any potion or herbal remedies to treat Panduma.

Nondo with his *gwika* leaf would surely heal him, thought Porugl. But seeking Nondo posed a problem. He couldn't return to the Underworld and wondered if another route existed to get Nondo's attention. The *gigl* would not be roaming the Akenku lands. *Gigl* didn't forage in battle ridden lands. Other unknown spirits would be there, consuming and adding to the fear and fright the battle had brought.

Porugl sat beside Panduma, waiting for dawn to break, and gazed at the sky. Immediately, thoughts of Maie hit him. The voices of the elders came into his mind, rudely interrupting his sweet thoughts of his wife. He couldn't think about his wife now. He had to think about the dawning day. He saw Panduma shivering but could not do anything. He hoped that he had thought everything through.

The uproar confirmed the Kumoku and Tambaiku would be crossing over the river with determination more than ever to finish what they started. They would not hold back and bring their full arsenal of weapons, seasoned warriors, and to unleash Irawam Toglkumba.

Porugl presented to his warriors an unorthodox battle plan and made sure everyone understood their part. They went over their plan many times. Everyone knew that Porugl feared no one, but now the young warriors recognized him as a brilliant tactician. They considered his battle strategies and agreed he had the right to take over as Chief of Akenku after his grandfather.

The boys didn't have the privilege of seeing Kande Kumugl in action before coming to the end of his reign. They heard the stories of his heroics from their parents at home. They worked tirelessly in the night to set up their plan. It was complete and ready for action before the new day dawned. Porugl knew the Kumoku and Tambaiku would throw everything at them. He didn't sleep much, running the situations again and again in his mind to make sure he anticipated correctly what would happen. He went with Panduma to the other warriors.

"Follow what we discussed and we will be alright.

Whatever happens, we will meet at Bindekai if we get separated."

A loud commotion came across the river as men shouted at each other in angry voices. Shortly after, a thunderous war cry came across. The echoes of their voices sent shivers through everyone who heard them. The different tribes and villages in all of Kondaland came out of their houses and stood at strategic points to see the battle take place. Their leaders strictly advised them that no warrior would go into the fight. They would be spectators. The leaders feared that this could escalate into something bigger involving all tribes in Kondaland and had the potential to spill forth into Koraland. The river naturally divided the tribes. All tribes on Akenku's side rooted for them, while tribes on the Kumoku side wanted to see the complete annihilation of Akenku.

Waine looked at Porugl. He was shaking and Porugl grabbed his arm.

"Courage, my brother forever. Courage wins wars, not numbers," said Porugl.

"Courage wins wars, not numbers," said Waine, trying to sound confident.

These words really sunk into the young warriors. They heard it countless times over and over again from the elders and seasoned warriors. The impact didn't establish itself in their minds until this very moment. The words described an article of life in the Akenku tribe and not some loose utterance someone adopted from the wayside. Experience created these words, passed down from generation to generation even before the time of Kande Kumugl.

They clung together in a final embrace. The same feelings they had felt with the entire tribe came flooding back. They waited for the Kumoku and Tambaiku advance war party, camouflaged by the thick overgrowth near the battlefront.

The minions plied their trade on Porugl as he waited.

"You will die today," they whispered.

Porugl heard the voice and looked around.

"What is it?" said Waine.

'Did you hear something?"

"What thing?"

Waine shook his head.

"They will kill your wife and your mother if you do not return now," they uttered.

"Get away from me," said Porugl and looked around.

"Evil spirits are with us, Porugl, focus," said Ningir.

"We are going to battle evil spirits as well," said Waine.

"Oh mighty Kekemba, take these spirits away," cried Porugl.

No Kekemba came around. But when Kimin-ege, Gurr-toki and Agandua heard Kekemba's name, they fled.

"Shhh, they are coming," said Ningir.

The Tambaiku and Kumoku cautiously crossed the river into Gandia. Ten shields appeared and led the advance party into the battlegrounds. Bindi Kumugl and Dee Kumugl walked a distance from the shields, with Irawam Toglkumba in tow. The giant grunted and said something which resembled Porugl's name.

"Pougl, Pougl," he grunted. "Pougl, Pougl."

"Yes, I know. You will have him today. You will drink his blood before my very eyes," assured Bindi Kumugl.

"Pougl, Pougl," Toglkumba kept grunting even more loudly in a deep voice.

Dee Kumugl heard what Bindi Kumugl said to Toglkumba and realized he knew the truth.

"You lied to me, for that, when we return, all the Kumoku lands and the Akenku lands will be mine."

Dee Kumugl didn't respond.

"I killed you in an ambush, you killed me in an ambush. Now come forward and fight like a man," shouted one of the elders behind the line of shields.

"Hear me, Akenku, be a man and come and fight, or are you a coward? We know that your women and children are with the Wakiku. Once we finish with you, we will go up to Bogl. If you value them, you should come out now and fight," continued the same elder.

"Now," said Porugl.

He and three warriors ran across the battlefield with their shields to the place they had prepared. Panduma struggled to catch up.

"They must have been sleeping," said one of the Kumoku warriors. The warriors laughed loudly.

Dee Kumugl studied the young warriors as they went about setting themselves up and said, "What are they doing? They look young."

"Is that all?" asked Bindi Kumugl, and he snickered.

"This is too easy. Others could be in hiding. It is a trap," said Dee Kumugl.

Bindi Kumugl glared at Dee Kumugl, his blood already boiling.

"If you say, 'It's a trap', one more time, I will kill you and feed you to Irawam Toglkumba."

He was still looking at Dee Kumugl after he said it. Dee Kumugl didn't turn around or show any reaction. He heard it and kept looking ahead. The advance party watched the two shields and wondered why the third shield didn't come up to the front.

"Enough of wasting time, flank them," shouted Bindi Kumugl.

The shields on the outer edges moved around. Porugl said this would happen. The men bearing the shields and those behind in the cover of the shields saw the four young warriors and already underestimated them. The attentiveness of the enemy war party subsided when they saw the four young men and compared them to their horde of seasoned warriors. Porugl also counted on that reaction from the war party.

"Cautiously men, cautiously," said an aged, seasoned warrior. "These kids couldn't have slaughtered our warriors yesterday.

They anticipated that any time during the battle, the real Akenku force would attack. This brought uncertainty and doubt as they began to enclose the young warriors.

"That is exactly what we want them to do," Porugl had

explained.

Bindi Kumugl saw the young warriors concentrate their arrows on one side of the approaching line of shields while the other side was advancing freely. This is going to be fast, he thought and smiled to himself. Meanwhile, Toglkumba continued grunting in the background, eager to run into battle.

The fast-moving line of shields got dangerously close when there was a sudden crash plunging them into the earth. Several warriors tried to get out of the pit, but arrows ended their lives swiftly. Two men in the pit screamed in pain as sharp, pointed stumps drove into them, spurting out their intestines. When the other flanking shields saw this, they stopped their advance and stood undecided if they should continue.

"Why are you stopping" yelled, Bindi Kumugl, who was getting restless. "Keep going."

The warriors didn't heed his command and remained stationary. They had seen many of them slaughtered yesterday, and they were all quite sure the main Akenku war party was using these young warriors as bait to lure them in. They didn't to want to experience the next surprise after witnessing what had happened. They saw fours shields destroyed and eight warriors killed in that move by the young Akenku warriors.

Even the *yer arai* being fired by the enemy shooters were not hitting their mark. The placement of the three shields sheltered Waine, Panduma, and Ningir from the hail of assault arrows. Two shields faced the enemy slanting backwards. They wedged the lower ends of the shields into a dip already dug into the ground. A big branch supported the two shields, and both were rock steady. They had rehearsed it in the night already and replayed it. They placed the third behind the two front shields slanted forward. This reduced the opening above. Porugl expected the Kumoku and Tambaiku to let loose a fury of *yer arai* or the deadly silent assault arrows. He figured that for their assault arrows to be threatening; the shooters had to stand way back across the river and up towards Kumoku land. Right now, the shooters stood behind the shields, giving them little range and reducing chances of any impact. The four young warriors would execute the next part of their plan without having to worry about the deadly *yer arai* from above and concentrate on engaging the front assault team. Porugl stood at the back behind his own shield and directing his arrows to the line of shields that stopped.

Some of the shooters realized this and moved further away from the shields. One of the marksmen got a good vantage point on Porugl and let loose one arrow straight towards him. In the midst of dodging arrows, Porugl caught sight of a fly right in front of him. At that moment, words of an elder he heard in the *yal yungu* came to him.

"In battle, an arrow coming straight at you will look like a fly. If you see a fly in front of you, get out of its way."

Porugl thrust himself away, missing the arrow only

barely. The arrow shot into the ground, its tail vibrating. He got up and raced to the man who nearly killed him. The warrior let loose another set of arrows, but in his rush and fear, did a poor job. This attracted all the shooters who fired repeatedly at Porugl.

"Kill him," screamed Bindi Kumugl and Dee Kumugl together.

Irawam Toglkumba became agitated and pleaded to be released, but Bindi Kumugl kept him at bay.

Porugl could have killed the man, but the hail of arrows stopped his advance and he took cover behind a tree. A group of warriors bearing axes and spears moved towards Porugl. The young warriors saw the movement and concentrated their arrows on them.

"Why is the front assault team not moving?" yelled Bindi Kumugl. "What is happening?"

"He is only one man," screamed Dee Kumugl.

The warriors spread out quickly towards Porugl. They were cautious of arrows coming from the young warriors.

"Break those two shields down," ordered Bindi Kumugl, but still, the line of shields maintained their stance.

Warriors behind the line of shields lost their enthusiasm and concentration. Moments ago, they saw four young men, who didn't look like they had any battle experience, take down eight seasoned warriors already. They refused to take a step further, suspecting that more traps lay ahead. They figured the main Akenku war party would execute them if they moved forward. While it seemed the right time in battle to make a charge, they didn't want to be caught out by the Akenku. The loss suffered yesterday and today couldn't have been the work of four boys. Many scenarios played on their minds, just as Porugl had intended. Other seasoned warriors knew how cunning and brave the Akenku could be.

Panduma saw the warriors about to isolate Porugl from them. They focused on him. If they killed him, then all their efforts would count for nothing. Bindi Kumugl would take over all of Kondaland, thought Panduma. Whatever happens, Porugl had to be alive for the tribe to survive. Porugl had to get back for the next play to take place. Panduma stood up with renewed energy and held his shield upright. He ignored the sharp pain he felt.

"What are you doing?" said Waine, in the midst of firing arrows.

"Courage wins battles, not numbers," he said. "I'm putting the next phase of the plan into motion."

"No, no, we have to wait for Porugl," said Ningir, but Panduma stepped out, already charging to the enemy.

The lone running shield startled the warriors, albeit its wobbly movement, as Panduma tried to contain the pain.

"This is the beginning of another trick," said a seasoned warrior behind the shields.

The shields came together and strengthened their defensive line. The attack on Porugl paused as the enemy warriors sighted the lone shield moving quickly. Panduma had no intention of stopping, and he crashed his shield into theirs. The line was solid, and he bounced back. Two warriors came out between the shields with their axes, but arrows from Waine and Ningir drove them back. While retreating to his side of the battle front, he called out to Irawam Toglkumba, taunting him. He danced and pranced around in front of the enemy while avoiding the arrows and spears hurled at him. For that moment, he forgot about his pain. The Kumoku and Tambaiku still didn't want to advance out to Panduma without the cover of their shields. Their shield men didn't want to fall into another Akenku trap, so they stood their ground. Some enemy warriors made moves to run at Panduma and hack him to death, but arrows from Ningir and Waine discouraged them.

Waine and Ningir heard hard knocks intermittently on their shields made by the *yer arai*. The shooters were in good range and would not stop. An arrow landed between Waine and Ningir, and they both jolted.

"If we have to do anything it has to be now, I'm running out," said Waine, examining his quiver.

Porugl appreciated what Panduma was doing and brought forward the next part of their battle scheme.

"One-eyed son of a dog, where are you?" he called loudly, seeing Irawam Toglkumba at the back and using his shield as cover.

Irawam Toglkumba seethed with rage at hearing Panduma.

'You are the son of a dog, a kumo kwimbo!" he screamed.

Irawam Toglkumba could not take it anymore when

he heard Panduma telling him that his mother had sexual relations with a dog. He broke ranks, smashing the shields in front and bumping aside the warriors like leaves. Bindi Kumugl called to Irawam Toglkumba at the top of his voice, but the one-eyed giant continued to run ferociously towards Panduma. He had one thing on his mind - eating this pest before anything else.

That was the fastest Bindi Kumugl saw Irawam Toglkumba sprint. With Toglkumba already engaged in the battle, Bindi Kumugl had no choice but to push further.

'Warriors spread out and the shield line move ahead," he said.

He sighed and thought about Goimbu.

They still didn't move, so he came up and swung his axe wildly at the men behind the shields. Immediately, the warriors began spreading out, and the shields moved forward.

With the attention now on Panduma and Irawam Toglkumba, Porugl took the opportunity and sprinted back behind his two shield men. There was a loud uproar of commotion from the enemy lines as Irawam Toglkumba lunged forward after Panduma. A hail of arrows from the Kumoku and Tambaiku followed suit. The shield line was moving faster, and the warriors quickened their pace. The two Akenku young men holding the shields prepared to open up for Panduma as he raced back. Timing was of essence as they got ready for Panduma's arrival and that of the giant. They saw the enemy warriors spreading out and the advancing line of shields.

"Open up," shouted Panduma.

Waine and Ningir opened their shields. Toglkumba saw the young warrior scuttling behind and increased his pace. Each step from Toglkumba took two from Panduma. Toglkumba ran with a speed enough to bump over a full-grown tree. The two shields didn't close after Panduma passed. Toglkumba didn't bother. If they did, he would just run over them. The earth shook as the giant charged through. Panduma could feel the monstrosity bearing down on him. He would not execute the plan well if he changed his direction, so he kept running in the same direction. Waine and Ningir closed the shields behind as the giant sped past. Everyone saw the giant's head and body suddenly disappearing behind the two shields. Waine and Ningir had their axes ready if the plan failed. Toglkumba kept going and reached out. At the exact spot where Panduma had to change direction, he stepped out of the way, but not quick enough. The giant's thick, calloused hands gripped his neck. Right then, a loud thud riveted the earth. Toglkumba let out a horrendous growl of pain. The advancing war party and the line of shields strained to see ahead. For a moment, their hail of arrows stopped. Everyone across Kondaland heard the beast's voice. Tribes rooting for Akenku cheered while the other tribes swore and hurled insults at them. They threatened to get weapons and cross over. The tribes told them to come.

"What's happening," yelled Bindi Kumugl. No one

responded. The events ahead took over their concentration.

The giant fell with a mighty crash into a bigger pit the boys prepared for him. The sharp stumps in the pit drove into the giants body. One stump split right through his thigh and another drove into his torso. The fall put Toglkumba off balance, and the inertia propelled his upper body forward with great force. As his huge head came down, Porugl rushed into him, driving a long sharp tree stump with all his strength and might into his windpipe. The stump entered with a sickening crunch and protruded out the other end. The Kumoku and the Tambaiku heard the sound the stump made, but it all happened behind the shields and no one really understood the cause. Toglkumba opened his mouth, but no sound came out. His tongue stuck out and the big eye was looking at Porugl in disbelief and fright. Porugl left the stump on the giant's neck and went to check Panduma. Toglkumba's hand had smashed him in the fall. He was bleeding heavily. Porugl looked at him and he looked up at Porugl. Waine and Ningir left their shields and came to him.

"Go," said Panduma, coughing up blood. "Go now," he said and tried to smile.

"My brother forever," said Porugl. Waine and Ningir echoed his words.

The Kumoku and Tambaiku all watched in awe and horror as Porugl and his young warriors brought down the monster; Irawam Toglkumba.

"What happened? Where is he?" shouted Bindi Kumugl.

"I don't know," said Dee Kumugl, and both men walked

to the front line of shields.

"We cannot see," said the one of the warriors, moving around to get a better view.

"They killed him, you idiots, attack!" screamed Bindi Kumugl and started swinging his axe at anyone.

"Porugl, we have to go," said Waine.

Porugl took one last look at Panduma. They would mourn him later after their retreat.

"Attack!" screamed Bindi Kumugl again.

The war party started moving in all directions. Warriors sprinted across the battlefield. They paused to see the monster with the stump stuck in his neck and his tongue sticking out. They felt scared to pursue the young warriors after witnessing this ghastly sight. Others kept running in the direction of the fleeing Akenku warriors. A couple of warriors secretly deserted the war party.

Toglkumba's ugly grimace shocked the advance war party. Each step they took brought them to uncertainty. They didn't know if Porugl really retreated. It could be another ploy to bring them further inland to kill them all. Dee Kumugl and Bindi Kumugl continued to berate the warriors, who hesitated.

Porugl and the two young warriors left their fallen brother and moved quickly back into the bushes. He whistled their secret whistle three times across the river and they continued running up towards to Bindekai.

The advancing war party heard the whistle and paused.

This is it, some of them thought. This is the signal for the next assault. The war party gathered around with bows and arrows out, looking attentively at the surroundings. Bindi Kumugl caught up to them.

"Enclose, Enclose! You idiots, Enclose!" he yelled.

The advancing shields halted and enclosed the warriors.

"Keep your eyes open. What's happening out there? Tell me what's happening?" said Bindi Kumugl.

Some of the shields were knocking against each other and causing a disturbing noise.

"Stop shaking you lousy excuse of a warrior," said Bindi Kumugl, but the knocking didn't stop.

They peered cautiously out of the spaces between the shields. Sweat flowed freely, making their hands and bodies wet. Bindi Kumugl and Dee Kumugl stood in the middle of the group, but both men didn't feel safe.

Bindi Kumugl then ordered two men to go and scout the surroundings. The cool wind crept in as the shields opened. They kept close to each other. A short moment passed when they returned with nothing serious to report. The shields relaxed a little, and the warriors came out, but still weary of the threat.

Porugl and the young warriors stopped moving. From amongst the leaves they saw the enemy come to a halt. A loud commotion began to increase in volume from behind the war party.

"Look, smoke," shouted one of the warriors, pointing to

the Kumoku village.

They all turned around. Thick smoke rose and increased in density. A handful of warriors dashed back, leaving their weapons and shields behind. Some retreated in fear, while others had a genuine reason to retreat. They had women, children and properties to protect. They took the opportunity.

"Come back here, it's a trap" said Bindi Kumugl.

Dee Kumugl opened his eyes really wide and stared at Bindi Kumugl. No words needed to be said. His face said it all.

"Some of you go back with Dee Kumugl to the village. The rest will pursue these little maggots with me," said Bindi Kumugl.

Dee Kumugl was relieved and returned to the village quickly with a group of warriors. He saw women and children crying as he entered.

Mange and Bauglo had sneaked into the Kumoku village the previous night. They watched the Kumoku and Tambaiku pick their dead along the banks of the river. Lots of people crowded outside their houses talking about the day. The two boys went into the crowd and mingled with them. No one paid any attention to two insignificant looking boys. Their faces were painted black, like all the male faces in the village. They lingered outside the *yal yungu*, when the discussions heated and avoided conversation. They made sure to keep their distance from the young Kumoku warriors. The two found a secluded spot by the ridge and spent the rest of the night there.

They watched the battle take place below the next day and sent silent prayers to their ancestors to protect Porugl and the others. The two waited in secret, and their impatience grew when they heard the secret whistle. The first part of the plan had worked and they would execute the next part. Mange and Bauglo ran down into the village. The women and children all had their eyes on the battlefield. A few seasoned warriors stood watch with a group of young warriors like themselves. Mange crept into the first house and lit it on fire. Bauglo did the same to another house and then another house. By the time the people in the village realized, fire and smoke consumed many houses. This caught the women and children by surprise and they rushed about frantically.

"The Akenku are coming, the Akenku are coming, run," shouted the both of them, pointing to the smoke and running in the opposite direction.

The few warriors present took positions with their arrows pointed in the direction of the smoke. One of them told a small boy to go down and tell the warriors. Meanwhile, Mange and Bauglo continued to burn houses, creating a lot of confusion. Bauglo spotted the *yal yungu* and knew he had to burn it down. If the *yal yungu* remained intact, the Kumoku would draw strength from it, regardless of the outcome. One of the warriors back tracked to find Bauglo lifting a flame to the *yal yungu*'s thatched roof and ran to Bauglo with his axe.

"They are here," shouted the warrior.

Bauglo avoided the first swing of the warrior's axe and fell down, dropping the flame. He got up quickly, and they scuffled. The Kumoku warrior put him to the ground again and searched for his axe. Another warrior came and swung his axe at Bauglo's head and missed as two arrows struck him. Mange came from behind, thrust his axe into the warrior's head, instantly killing him.

"Come on, it's done, let's go," said Mange.

"Wait, wait, let me burn this filth first," said Bauglo and lit the *yal yungu*.

Bindi Kumugl and his war party didn't spot Porugl and his warriors. They waited for their next orders, hoping to return. The warriors felt down and defeated beyond relief. The people would mock their lineage and belittled them as long as the memory of this defeat existed. Some felt like crying. Others felt like just dropping everything and running away. They had been outclassed and outmaneuvered by a group of young men. One lay dead with Toglkumba. The previous victory over the Akenku would count for nothing. The smoke coming from their village was increasing in its thickness. Porugl and his warriors had achieved what they came to do.

"They have gone. We will never be able to find them. This is their land," said one of the warriors.

"Our houses are burning. We need to go back," said

another and started walking.

Still no word came from Bindi Kumugl. His two enforcers, Toglkumba and Goimbu, lay rotting in the earth. All this started when he married Dengg, he thought.

"Dengg," he shouted and ran back to the Kumoku village.

Everyone in Dawake, had a sullen face. Many of the warriors who had previously engaged enthusiastically in courting died in battle. The sun hid from the village and the dying smoke from the burnt houses refused to subside. They all sat in the central part of the village. Women rubbed mud over their faces and bodies and wept. They rolled around on the ground and continued to wail. The *yal yungu* that had stood during the time of Dee Kumugl's grandfather now lay waste in a pile of cinder. Dee Kumugl stood in front, looking lost, and rubbed the ashes on his face. The implications of what had happened and the repercussions would reverberate for generations. All throughout the history of the Kumoku, they had faced several defeats in warfare with the surrounding tribes. But never had they lost their *yal yungu*. In Kondaland, losing a *yal yungu* meant losing your identity, your pride, your history and your respect - the only thing worse than death.

The Akenku didn't fret too much about losing their *yal yungu* because the Kumoku had been treacherous and ambushed them. This argument didn't suffice for the Kumoku. The whole land would know Dee Kumugl as the man who lost the tribe and its highest institution of power. Dee Kumugl understood that recovery from this would not happen, ever.

The man sitting next to Dee Kumugl didn't reflect the proud and boisterous Bindi Kumugl, who had only recently charged into the welcome reception held by the Dawake village. During the welcome celebrations, he boasted a lot. His warriors came fully armed and, on the prowl, to kill and destroy anything in their path. He had Goimbu, his trustworthy commander, and most of all, he had Irawam Toglkumba. No one challenged his right to rule the lands. That man didn't exist anymore. He sat there for hours, staring blankly into nowhere, lost in his misery. Women who lost husbands, sons and possessions continued to mourn. Where is this boy? He thought. As if in answering his own question, thoughts began filling up in his mind. Bindi Kumugl couldn't resist the urge to sleep and drifted off. It didn't take too long before Gurr-toki and Agandua convinced Bindi Kumugl he needed to finish off what he started.

He looked up occasionally, hoping that Dengg would come and share his sorrows. Nobody came close to him. He searched the women's faces, but they kept weeping. He waited. He would ask about Dengg when one of them stopped. No one was watching him like they did previously. Each was lost in their own grief. He saw a woman who was sobbing by herself and thought she had stopped. He went over to her and sat beside her. The woman thought he came over to share her grief and she hugged him and began wailing loudly. All the women saw them and increased their wailing. Bindi Kumugl sat there hugging her, waiting for her to finish. He moved and the woman let go of him.

"My sister," he said. "Have you seen Dengg?"

"What?" said the woman.

"I said have you seen Dengg—"

"Eeepahh," screamed the woman. "We have lost everything and all you can think of is that bitch, it's because of you that we are like this, you took her into the *yal yungu* and defiled it, you old good-for-nothing chief, why did you come here?"

The other woman started coming closer and asked the women what Bindi Kumugl said. He sat there with his head between his hands, knowing that he should not have asked this question.

"This guy wants to know where Dengg is. What kind of chief is this guy?" she said.

All the women turned their attention to him, called him names, swore at him and spat on him. One of the women went and got a big stick and wanted to bang his head when Dee Kumugl stopped them.

"All of us are suffering. Just let him be," said Dee Kumugl.

"Are you going to get one of our young girls and give her to him now?" said one of the women.

"Yes, like you did with Dengg," said another. "He cannot go one night without Dengg, so are you going to?"

Yes, tell us shouted all the women. They moved closer to

him with rock and stick in their hands.

"Hey hey, calm down," he said.

"Just tell us," shouted the first woman.

"No," said Dee Kumugl.

"I saw Dengg making her way to Bogl. She has gone to become Porugl's second wife," said another woman. They all laughed.

"Come, let's go," said Dee Kumugl.

Reports came that a combined troupe of Kumoku and Tambaiku warriors struggled to bring Irawam Toglkumba's body back. A filthy stench choked the men. They tried all sorts of ways, but the body didn't budge. Some men suggested leaving it. Dee Kumugl ordered everyone; men, women and children to go down and haul Irawam Toglkumba's body. Bindi Kumugl instructed them to burn all the bodies; Toglkumba included. Many in the village didn't like it. They stood at a distance and watched when a runner came and informed him that the northern tribes sympathized with him.

These tribes had built a long and lasting relationship with the Tambaiku and Kumoku and naturally felt drawn in. Despite being less, the Akenku inhabited the most fertile lands and had more than any other tribe. Other tribes hated them for this. A great commotion spread across the land and many of these tribes made their way to Dawake.

Bindi Kumugl made known his intentions to Dee Kumugl and announced that all tribes who he helped previously had to repay their debt in this conflict. He told the Kumoku; he had to be close with his brothers, with one last stand against Akenku and all their allies. They would start their raid on Daneku. He couldn't return with that kind of blood on his hand, so he had no choice but to pursue the reason for him coming down in the first place.

13

Nondo The Dwarf

G oglko returned to the Underworld after he witnessed Porugl slaying the giant. There was a loud rapture of voices when he broke the news to the beings and the whole cavern shook.

"Silence" said Goglko.

"The balance of life is hanging in the air. Kerwanba, the ancient serpent and ruler of the Underworld, has taken part in the war above. She will either retreat in shame after failing again or she will break the balance herself. You all know what happens when the balance is broken."

The creatures and beings in the realm became animated.

"We don't know what will happen now. Be on your guard, the serpent will be coming,"he said.

Nondo came out of Milime's abode and listened. Nondo still had the *gwika* leaf that Porugl had brought to him. He wondered if Porugl needed its healing powers, with all the fighting going on. Nondo couldn't help but think that he had to go above to the Outerworld and tell Porugl about the great secret. There was treachery in the way he had seen the old serpent talking to Kewand Kumugl. The whole cavern heard what Kewand Kumugl said when Kerwanba approached him. Nondo sensed betrayal in Kewand Kumugl. He had to warn Porugl about Kewand Kumugl. Creatures in the cavern had changed in their attitude toward Kewand Kumugl. They used to be carefree around him, but now they hesitated to communicate with him. Nondo became uneasy around Kewand Kumugl. Milime had told Nondo that Kewand Kumugl wanted to go to the Outerworld and she helped him. Nondo berated Milime.

"You should have told me first. If he comes to ask again, tell him no," said Nondo.

Nondo knew Kewand Kumugl went up to the Outerworld for a reason.

"I have to go" said Nondo to Milime.

"Where?" Milime said quickly.

"I just have to go." Nondo didn't trust Milime to keep his whereabouts a secret. She would definitely tell Kewand Kumugl if he asked.

"I have to go check some clients."

"Now? When the Outerworld is in havoc and affecting every being in the Underworld, you want to go now?" asked Milime

"Yes now, if I don't use the gwika leaf, its powers will subside. You know that, Milime, stop acting like a child," said Nondo.

The leaf never lost its powers. Milime didn't know this fact about the *gwika* leaf. First, he had to do something. He had to go into the dwarf realm.

"Aaahhh, the missing one returns," said one of the dwarves, who was stationed outside Mando's abode.

Nondo had been missing in the dwarf realm for a while now after Porugl gave him the *gwika* leaf. No one in the dwarf realm knew that Porugl had given it to him. The returning dwarves reported that a human, by the name of Porugl, had come and stolen the *gwika* leaf.

"The coward Porugl snatched the leaf from me," said one of the dwarves.

"The underling is a thief. He robbed us of the *gwika* leaf and ran like a rat," said another.

Suddenly every dwarf wanted to talk, filling the hollow cavern with their voices. The dwarves believed this was an act of aggression and ceased all their dealings with the Outerworld. They demanded that the *gwika* leaf be returned to them at once.

The *gwika* leaf, or the enhancer as it was commonly known in the realms, was a well traded item. A tiny piece of the *gwika* leaf was worth more to the dwarf than the Outerworld could imagine, because it was the most powerful healing remedy. The *gwika* leaf was crushed into fine powder and mixed with limestone and other ingredients. The powder sparkled when it was sprinkled. The intensity of the sparkle indicated its strength and was the basis of its value. The fine dust, called *sperraro*, was used to enhance any spell.

The Outerworld sought it from witch doctors who procured it from the dwarves. There was no other traded item like *sperraro*. It was the currency of the Underworld. Its powder was diluted again and again and by the time it hit the streets of the other realms, it contained only a glimmer of its true power. Nonetheless, it was a hotly traded item and a central focus of business by the dwarves. Not only was the *gwika* leaf used to heal injuries and sickness, but to enhance any spell or incantation that was evoked. Without this leaf, trading by the dwarves was difficult. The *gwika* tree releases one leaf after a very long time. All business conducted by the dwarves was coming to a halt. Witchdoctors in the Outerworld ran out of their supply of magical herbs. People who got sick or sustained life-threatening injuries ended up dying. Evil spirits couldn't be repelled and continued to haunt and taunt people in the Outerworld. Life, both in the Outerworld and the Underworld, was deeply affected by the absence of the gwika leaf.

Little did they know that the *gwika* leaf was with Nondo. He heard the vibrations of his name coming through and knew the dwarf realm was out to get him. Since that time, rarely did Nondo come out of his abode. Milime went out and foraged for the both of them. Nondo was content with where he was. Even if anything happened to him, he had the new *gwika* leaf, which was still intact. He would be able to sustain or heal himself if he faced any attack.

"Is he in?" asked Nondo.

"We haven't seen you since the underling stole the *gwika* leaf."

Nondo looked at Gindo.

"Is Mando in?" he asked again.

"Did you have anything to do with it?" asked Gindo.

Nondo made an attempt to go past the guard.

"Yes, he is in. You better have a good explanation for your absence…traitor."

Mando, the chief dwarf in the dwarf realm, lay on his bed. Mando came to the dwarf realm before any other dwarf. Most of the dwarves could not recall anyone before Mando.

"You have been gone for a while," said Mando.

"Yes, I—"

"You don't have to tell me. I know we are still watching, or have you forgotten?"

'No, Chief Mando.'

"There is something bothering you."

"I came to ask you, to tell you, I am going to Porugl. I came to seek your permission."

"You know, the Underworld and Outerworld cannot interact in the manner you seek."

"Yes, I know, but Kerwanba might break the balance of life," said Nondo. "I am trying to do my part to restore the balance."

"Huh? What can you do? Don't you think I know what she has done?" said Mando in a louder voice.

"I'm sorry," said Nondo. "There is something about this boy. I have to go and warn him."

"You really like this boy."

"I believe he is the only one to keep the balance. That's why I have to help him, otherwise you know what will happen."

"You are insulting me as if I do not know the consequences of breaking the balance between the Underworld and the Outerworld. Your free pass has expired. Fail this task and you will never return to the Underworld. I will strip you of all your powers, relieve you of your possessions, including Milime, and left out there. And you know what happens to dwarves in the Outerworld without their powers? You have been away from your realm for far too long. Maybe you want to start your own domain. But if it has something to do with the *gwika* leaf, I will let you go. But before that, you must know this."

He beckoned Nondo to come closer and in whispers told Nondo of the deep dark secret that Kerwanba kept. Nondo didn't say anything and focused all the way to the end.

"She has brought this upon herself. Now go," said Mando.

"I am sorry for being away too long. Here is a parting gift to the realm…I go to the Outerworld now."

Nondo pinched the tip of the gwika leaf and put it in his pouch and left the rest beside Mando. The dwarf chief didn't say anything, nor did he turn around. He smiled and continued sleeping.

14

A Painful Lesson

Kerwanba waited for her minions to report on the news that Irawam Toglkumba had killed Porugl. The minions shuddered. Their lives would end now. She would know what happened eventually and bite them with her poisonous fangs. The thought made them cringe.

"We have to tell her," said Kimin-ege.

"Yes, you tell her," said Agandua.

"No, you tell her," said Kimin-ege.

"We will all tell her," shouted Gurr-toki.

The uproar caused by the beings in Goglko's realm had disturbed her. She opened an eyelid lazily, waiting for more vibrations to come in. She knew the epicenter of the tremor. That particular realm found every opportunity to get on her nerves. They seemed to be the ones always noisy, always vocal, always celebrating, and always in defiance. They celebrated when Porugl entered. They started the wave of rumours that Porugl had beaten her at the cliffs of Sikewake. They roared with hope when Porugl ended Dingan's life. They fell silent when the Kumoku and Tambaiku killed so many Akenku warriors and ravaged their lands. And now they shook every crevice and rock formation in the Underworld with their jubilation. Something had triggered this reaction. The after effects of the pandemonium didn't end. She listened attentively to the vibrations.

"Toglkumba is..." but the vibrations faded away.

Then came another wave.

"Porugl killed the..." and the voices ebbed away.

"...will Kerwanba do...?"

Still, she couldn't get complete sentences and stuck her ear to the rock walls. All of a sudden, the voices came well and truly clear along the cave walls, and the vibrations increased in intensity as it came closer. She didn't believe what she heard. A sudden muscular spasm hit her and her head and her tail bumped the cave walls loudly. Pieces of rock fell as shivers kept resonating along the length and breadth of her domain.

Then it came through. She didn't struggle to hear. The loud and boisterous proclamation hit her like a big rock. It bounced off the walls, into the deep dark crevices and entered all the realms. Some realms rejoiced while others feared what would happen next. A great commotion stirred in the Underworld.

"Irawàm Toglkumba is dead!" came the tremors again and again.

The words drove itself deep into her mind. She tried to hold the words at bay in her mind, but they kept on protruding and probing until they reached the depths of her being. And from there, what resonated back frightened the ancient serpent. The words gorged her mind as it made its way out from where a deep, dark secret lay hidden. A door to her sub-conscious tucked away under eons of time, now opened up.

"When the balance is broken, there is only one outcome," came the voice in her mind.

"No wait," said the serpent, gathering herself. "But I haven't broken the balance yet."

She looked around to see if anyone noticed her speaking to herself. In her mind, she knew exactly the origin of these words, and yet she forced her mind to block it out. The more she tried, the stronger the words came to her. She tried to shake the thoughts off, but it remained just as real as the cave walls of her domain.

"Minions!" she bellowed.

Her voice echoed throughout the holes and cervices seeping into all the realms. Creatures and beings felt the impact and stopped and scurried back into their abodes. She unwound herself and looked around. The forked tongue moved quickly in and out of her mouth. Kimin-ege, Agandua and Gurr-toki all heard her. The minions knew she would inflict in them a lifetime of pain. They assembled in front of her slowly and shaking.

"Queen of the deep dark, we are here," said Kimin-ege timidly.

"You scum, get out here and let me see you."

The three came out and moved forward towards the great snake.

"What is this I hear?"

"Ancient one, what did you hear?" asked Agandua.

"Is Porugl dead?"

"Queen of the deep dark, we saw Irawam Toglkumba grab Porugl, that's the last we saw," said Kimin-ege.

"And what of Irawam Toglkumba?"

"He killed Porugl, then the Akenku attacked him. Both Toglkumba and Porugl are dead."

Kimin-ege was not ready to suffer pain. She had already witnessed the lifetime of pain the serpent's deadly venom could induce. Kimin-ege told Kerwanba that they would have stayed around to bring Porugl's head back but had to flee when a Kekemba came around, circling above. This tricky revelation came to Kimin-ege only just then. The other two minions looked nervously at each other. Kimin-ege lied to Kerwanba's face. They had no choice but to follow Kimin-ege's lead. Irawam Toglkumba did grab someone. They knew very well it was the injured young warrior, but it could be a point to argue if Kerwanba later found out the truth. Kimin-ege would say they thought Irawam Toglkumba grabbed Porugl.

The age old serpent considered them for a while. The cool cave didn't stop the three from sweating under the glare of Kerwanba's angry red eyes. Kerwanba didn't take any chances. She would find out for herself. Before going up to the Outerworld, she had to teach them a lesson they would never forget. She had endured enough shame, humiliation and defeat to last her a lifetime many times over. This time, it was going to be different.

"You lie," said Kerwanba, and her forked tongue lunged out, grabbing Kimin-ege.

"My dark queen," screamed Kimin-ege.

The ancient serpent slowly pulled Kimin-ege towards her ghastly fangs. Kimin-ege struggled against the forked tongue. She begged Kerwanba and pleaded for her life, but the forked tongue brought her closer and closer to the serpent's deadly fangs. Gurr-toki and Agandua saw the clear poison squirting out of her fangs. Kimin-ege moved and writhed, unable to break free and let out a deathly scream as Kerwanba bit her, releasing her vile venom. Kerwanba let Kimin-ege drop to the rock floor, writhing in pain. Gurr-toki and Agandua watched in horror as the venom made its way into Kimin-ege's body. Kimin-ege twisted and turned on the rock floor, moaning in agony. Spit already formed in her mouth and her eyes moved without control. Creatures and beings in the different realms knew another had been bitten.

"I have one more thing for you to do. Now take Kimin-ege away. Don't come back if it is not done," she said.

Gurr-toki and Agandua responded quickly. They hauled Kimin-ege into their abode and laid her down. No potion or healing would be able to save Kimin-ege. Once out of

Kerwanba's hearing, Agandua and Gurr-toki did what Kimin-ege asked.

~

"Kewand Kumugl, Lord of the Underworld," came a mocking voice from outside his abode. He could hear the minions laughing as he stepped out.

Kewand Kumugl hoped luring Porugl to the fight against Irawam Toglkumba had settled his end of the deal. He waited for Kerwanba to release him. Then he heard Goglko report that Porugl had slain Irawam Toglkumba. His head ached, knowing Kerwanba would call upon him again and again until she achieved her target. He had no choice. He would have to do her bidding or end up dead. And Kewand Kumugl chose to stay alive. He lived in the Underworld for so long. The Underworld had given him what the Outerworld didn't. He couldn't sacrifice his life for Porugl. His life turned upside down when Porugl arrived. He had good intentions to help the boy heal from his injuries. But now he regretted ever helping him. Now he would be part of the scheme to end Porugl's life. He wanted his wife, the *gigl ambu*, to return to the Underworld. As treacherous as it might seem, Kewand Kumugl grabbed the opportunity offered by Kerwanba.

"Porugl is still alive, you know that," said Agandua.

"And what about Irawam Toglkumba," asked Kewand Kumugl.

"That doesn't matter," Gurr-toki cut in. "The heiress of

the deep dark has summoned you for a specific task. She says that your wife will be granted an opening back into the Underworld if you complete this task."

"I did her bidding already," argued Kewand Kumugl.

"And you failed, Porugl is still alive, you know you will never escape Kerwanba, all of your underlings are bound to her, if Porugl lives, you die, if he dies we all live, it's as simple as that," said Agandua.

"Where is your other companion?" asked Kewand Kumugl

"You will share the same fate if you don't do what Kerwanba has ordered you to do," said Gurr-toki.

"The two of us will accompany you to the entrance of Wakiku."

15

The Final Encounter

Porugl, Waine and Ningir rested for a while. The thick white smoke coming from Dawake, the Kumoku village, had distracted the pursuing war party. Ningir had an arrow stuck in his forearm while Waine had one sticking into his thigh. Porugl had a deep hole in his foot. An arrow had landed on it. The jagged edges of the arrow ripped the flesh as he pulled it came out. All the action had distracted them from the pain. Now as they rested, the pain was making itself unbearable in the afternoon sun. The Kumoku practiced magic and sealed their arrows in spells. Anything that came into contact with their arrows would surely die. They had until the next day to find someone who could neutralize the toxin. The shade of the small trees didn't help and all of them felt hot. He looked down at his swollen foot. The other two still had the arrows stuck into them. They cut off the overhanging parts of the arrow.

"We said to meet at Bindekai. We will stay awhile and then go," he said.

"Porugl, we need to go all the way to Wakiku," said Ningir.

"We will go. We have to wait for Bauglo and Mange."

"I miss Panduma," said Waine.

"We all do," said Porugl. "He sacrificed his life for us."

The sun set and the three warriors limped and made their slow and painful journey to the foot of Bindekai. Porugl felt the pain growing. He had to figure out how they would find someone to treat them. He saw his foot and knew this would end up killing him. He had seen it happen before. Porugl could not wait to go to Wakiku. He had to do something now.

Someone tugged at Porugl's leg, waking him up.

"That's really nasty," said Nondo, pointing to Porugl's foot.

Porugl looked down at his foot, then at Nondo, still in a daze. The color had returned to his foot. Someone had cleaned his wound and covered it with some stuff that looked like leaves.

"You are not dreaming," said Nondo and touched his hand.

Porugl shivered at his touch and got up quickly.

"How did you come?" asked Porugl.

"You called," said Nondo.

"Did I call?"

"You did, but you were fast asleep when I came."

"Let me touch you to know I'm not dreaming."

"Get away from me," said Nondo playfully, and walked away.

"I took the arrows out of your friends as well. I have seen arrow wounds, but these Kumoku arrows, filthy and loaded with their spells and their poison tip."

"How is Milime?"

"She is…well you know how gigl ambus are, you were married to one of them once," said Nondo and he laughed.

Porugl laughed with him, despite the pain in his foot.

"How long have I been sleeping?

"Two days."

"Two days," exclaimed Porugl and got up.

"Easy Porugl, a Kumoku black tip arrow hit you. They dip their arrows in poison and unleash it with a spell. No one survives a *dinmbi* or black tip arrow. The gwika leaf took some time to suppress the chant and poison, but don't worry, I have cleaned and healed you."

Porugl could feel his foot was much lighter, and the aching subsided.

"I have to tell you something," said Nondo.

Just then, Ningir and Waine came.

"Porugl, your friend Nondo is really something," said Waine.

Ningir held up his arm and Waine showed the wound on his thigh.

"That's his gwika leaf," said Nondo, looking at Porugl.

"Really?" said Waine. "How come?"

"What, Porugl, you didn't tell them yet?" said Nondo, smiling.

Porugl just shook his head.

"Please tell us," the two boys begged.

Nondo told the two boys how Porugl had single-handedly held off a group of angry dwarves to bring the *gwika* leaf. The story amazed the two boys. The *gwika* tree and its healing leaf was a myth to ordinary villagers and now they came into contact with a dwarf and a *gwika* leaf. He held out the *sperraro* made from the *gwika* leaf for them to see.

Nondo remained with the boys during the night. He would take the night watch and be off in the morning. A rustling in the bushes nearby spooked Nondo, and he woke the boys. They heard a familiar whistle coming from the forest.

"It's Bauglo and Mange," said Porugl.

The two boys walked out into the open.

"Where is Panduma?" asked Mange.

Ningir shook his head and Mange didn't ask anymore. Nondo appeared and gave them a fright. This would be the first time for Mange and Bauglo to see a dwarf.

"Here is my friend Nondo." said Porugl.

"Tatatatat, I am not his friend," said Nondo, smiling.

Nondo watched as the boys ate their sweet potatoes.

"We couldn't come earlier because they have blocked all the passages. They are keeping an eye on all tracks and roads in and out of Kondaland. What's more, all the tribes on that side of the river are amassing. All who had a grievance with the Akenku in the past have now joined forces with what is remaining of the Tambaiku and Kumoku," said Bauglo.

Then Mange described how he saw runners going in and out of Dawake.

"But it's more than that," added Bauglo. "Evil forces are at work now. The *kumo kwimbos* are amassing with meetings every night on the other side of the Bindekai peak. We met two nomads who told us of these nightly seances that the warlocks and witches held. They told us to be very careful."

"It's Kerwanba," said Nondo.

Suddenly everything went really quiet and the dark patches of the forest came out to spook them. They glanced at Nondo to continue, but Nondo himself regretted that he mentioned the name, didn't want to continue.

"Nondo continue," said Porugl.

Nondo got down and whispered.

"She is the source of the powers of all *kumo kwimbos*. If we threaten her existence, we threaten their existence as well. They will rally for her. That's all I can say for now. Bindi Kumugl follows a generation of *kumo kwimbos*. He is Chief of Tambaiku and king of all *kumo kwimbos* in the land, a title he sold his soul for. Some say that he slept with Kerwanba on the promise of a long life and dominance in the land. She bore him a son, Irawam Toglkumba. That other story about Irawam Toglkumba's origins is a lie to hide the one-eyed giant's true origins."

Porugl felt nauseous after hearing what Nondo said. This would be something unheard of in all the lands and realms. If the Underworld knew such a story, it would cause havoc. Porugl and his warriors now understood why these tribes easily pledged their allegiance. No other being other than Kerwanba could evoke so many tribes to join in the campaign against the Akenku.

Not only would they attack Akenku, but any other tribe thought to be its ally. All of Porugl's senses started working overtime thinking about all the tribes and villages the conflict would affect. The first village and tribe to be attacked would be the Daneku. The Akenku and Daneku became allies after the first and only battle between them, a long time ago. They vowed never to engage in war again and this pact still remains. He thought of the beautiful young girl from Daneku he had courted some time ago.

After the Daneku, the northern tribes would attack the Wakiku, Endaku, and Kumanku. Once the confrontation reached the Kombuglku, it would be over. The Kombuglku inhabited the extreme fringes of Kondaland, the last place where people spoke the common language. Koraland started where Kondaland ended. This conflict would devolve Kondaland back into a dark and dismal period. Such a period existed before all the ancestors. The elders didn't speak about the period. Probably because they didn't know much about it or they avoided talking about it. This dark period, known as the 'Kundawii', had a lot to do with the separation between mythical and magical creatures and humans.

Porugl felt a shudder run through his spine. The bits of information he gathered here and there told of a time when demons and evil spirits roamed the earth freely and openly. Kumo kwimbo, or humans possessed with evil spirits, practiced their sorcery out in public and in broad daylight, without shame or fear. Beings and spirits with all sorts of powers roamed the lands with man. In the battle for dominion, betrayal and treachery engulfed all ways of life. Men didn't trust other men, and spirit beings were suspicious of other beings and creatures. They formed their own allegiances when it suited them.

Tribes had to move constantly, travelling vast distances in short periods of time. Some tribes faded into oblivion, consumed completely by the Kundawii. Other tribes escaped the confrontations. A few tribes survived because of their bravery. This continued, and the spirit beings and creatures of the Underworld lived and breathed with men on the land, in the Outerworld. No permanent settlements or villages existed and tribes traveled from one spot to another. If they came across other tribes, they would battle each other without any reason. The remnants would either be scattered away into the outer reaches of the lands and from there, they would congregate again and continue to wander around and build their tribe again. The tumultuous period shaped life in Kondaland.

"Porugl, I have to tell you something. It's important. What I have to tell you is for you alone," said Nondo.

"Wait here," Porugl said to the others, and he went with Nondo up to the sacred burial ground.

Up at the peaks of Bindekai, Nondo told everything Porugl had to know about the deep, dark secret Kerwanba possessed. He also told Porugl to be careful and not to trust

Kewand Kumugl.

"Kewand Kumugl did come to visit me. He said he and Underworld would be behind me, but I didn't see them when we fought against the Tambaiku and the Kumokus," said Porugl.

"He lies," said Nondo.

"So are you saying Kewand Kumugl is helping Kerwanba?"

"I'm saying don't trust him."

"And why should I trust you?"

"I heard your call and came to heal you, and one more thing, two nights ago, you were calling in your dreams. When I came, you were crashing around in the bushes, the boys huddled together too frightened to do anything."

"What?"

"You jumped from tree to tree grunting like an animal, then you ran here and there, through the bushes and back, luckily you didn't run into a rock but you ran around wildly, your eyes were bloodshot red, we got really scared, I got scared imagine that, a dwarf doesn't get scared, and I was terrified at the way you looked at me, your eyes burned with hate, just like—"

"Stop."

"It seemed like you had lost your mind. I came and calmed you down. The boys saw me and went off in different directions. I had to bring them back with a soothing spell."

"Please, no more?"

"Porugl, when Dikamb died, she uttered a chant, a

powerful chant. It can only be reversed by her. Your life depends on it. You have to avenge your son and her and kill Kerwanba. If you don't, then you will slowly lose your mind and meet your fate. You don't know what I saw you do. It was frightening. It has already begun. The earlier you end Kerwanba, the better it is for you. See your legs and hands, see these bruises."

Porugl noticed fresh scratches on his arms and legs, which had already dried up.

"What is happening, Nondo?"

"That is the only way. You have to find Kerwanba and end her life. That is what Dikamb chanted, and that is the only way it will end."

There was a long moment of silence.

"That is the situation. There is no way of undoing this chant because Dikamb is dead. It cannot be undone," said Nondo.

"Why, Nondo, why did she bind me to such?"

"Porugl, we are not heartless beings in the Underworld, we have emotions, we love, we hate and we live and we die, Kerwanba took her firstborn, your son, it would have been done by anyone, I am sorry, I have to go back now."

"But if Irawam Toglkumba is Kerwanba's son, I killed her son. Shouldn't that release me from this irreversible bond to Dikamb?"

"That's not how it works. I have to go."

"Thank you for coming," said Porugl, "Will I see you

again?"

"I hope so. Oh, and I felt the presence of an Underworld being while you were running through the bushes. It smelled like Aglum, Kewand Kumugl's wife. She must be the one reporting back to the Underworld," said Nondo.

Porugl sat there looking over the land, thinking. The boys were getting restless when Porugl came down.

"We better leave for Bogl now," said one of them.

The boys arrived at the edge of the Kakam range in the afternoon. Nondo healed their injuries, but the exhaustion lingered. With no proper food and rest, it took a while before the boys came to the entrance of Bogl, the Wakiku village.

"Hold it," said a loud voice in the thick forest.

Porugl and his warriors stood still. A Wakiku warrior emerged out of the forests. A troupe of Wakiku came out of the bushes with arrows pointed at them.

"We are Akenku," said Waine. "Our tribe is in wandike with the Wakiku so we have come to join them."

"How do we know you are Akenku and not a scouting party from the Kumoku?" said the first Wakiku warrior in a loud voice.

"We are with Porugl," said Ningir.

The Wakiku warriors gave a puzzled expression on their faces and the atmosphere became tense.

"You lie, get down all of you, now," yelled the leader, and they pushed Porugl and the others to the ground.

The warriors bound the boys firmly with their hands

tied behind their back and placed them face down.

"My bow," said Porugl to the Wakiku warrior who had taken it from him. "If you do something to my bow, I'm going to kill you."

"Brothers, there is no need for this," said Waine. "We have just returned from fighting the Kumoku and the Tambaiku. We have slain the giant Irawam Toglkumba."

"You just shut your mouth," said the leader of the war party. "If you are here with Porugl, then who came yesterday?"

This strange news bewildered Porugl and the boys. The leader of the Wakiku war party whispered something to one of the warriors and he sped along the bush track while the other Wakiku warriors stood watch. Kondai, Anga Kumugl, Ormar and a group of seasoned warriors came.

'Porugl?" Kondai cried and hugged him, but Porugl felt her holding back. A strange feeling of uneasiness crept over everyone.

"You came yesterday. Where is Maie?"

Anga and his warriors stood watching.

"I didn't come yesterday," said Porugl. "Where is Maie?"

"What? I don't know what's happening. Is it really you?" she said, looking into Porugl's eyes.

Porugl became frustrated. A lot of questions started crowding his mind, and he felt dizzy.

"We just returned from destroying the Kumokus. Where is Maie?" asked Porugl.

"But you took Maie away yesterday," cried Kondai.

"Warriors, be alert," shouted Anga to the Wakiku warriors. "This could be some sort of sorcery."

At hearing this, the boys struggled against the ropes tying their hands and all of them protested.

"Who came and took her away then?" said Porugl, struggling against the ropes.

Kondai told the Wakiku warriors to bring some water. When a *gigl* took on human form, they never stepped over water, but around it. The warriors brought in a bundle of leaves.

"Step over it," Ormar ordered.

Porugl stepped over it.

"Untie them at once," said Anga Kumugl.

Kondai and Ormar hugged Porugl again, and the Wakiku apologized to the boys. Porugl told them about all that happened with the Kumoku and the Tambaiku.

"Someone or something just like you came yesterday and took your wife," said Kondai.

"We saw the smoke from here," said Anga Kumugl.

Kondai then related what happened. The imposter searched the village for Maie and came to Druwagle's house. He found Kondai and Maie working in a new garden nearby. Maie rejoiced and ran into the impersonator's arms. He then told Kondai, Druwagle and Damba that, to avoid any confrontation with the Kumoku, he had to leave with Maie. This made sense to Druwagle and Damba. The imposter said he came to get Maie, and that they would go to where it all began. It all sounded genuine. Maie got her bag happily, and they went. Kondai asked about the other boys and he said they waited at the entrance of the village.

All life drained from Porugl. He felt empty and void. He tried to figure out where this impersonator could have taken her. She must have sent her minions, or she must have sent Kewand Kumugl. It had to be Kewand Kumugl; he thought. After spending many seasons with Kewand Kumugl, he would know Porugl's mannerisms and how to respond to specific questions. It had to be Kewand Kumugl. The imposter had said 'the place where it all began'. The thought hung in his mind.

"I did think it was a bit strange, but didn't ask any more questions because Maie was so glad," said Kondai.

"You didn't come and see me about it," said Ormar to Kondai.

"We shall not waste any more time. A Wakiku search party will escort Porugl and look for Maie," said Anga Kumugl.

Kondai and the rest of the warriors returned to Bogl village with Ningir, Mange and Bauglo. Porugl said he would stay around and figure out where to start the search. Waine stayed with him.

Mange, Bauglo and Ningir arrived in Bogl, causing another stir in the village. The villagers surrounded the three boys to hear what happened with the Tambaiku and the Kumoku. After resting they came to the *yal yungu* and gave a recount of what happened. The reactions differed. Some said the Tambaiku and Kumoku might continue their war campaign in Wakiku lands. Others praised the boys for their bravery. While others said everyone should be alert.

Kimbi, Dingan's uncle, heard the discussion from the back. Kimbi left the *yal yungu* and hung around outside. Damba kept a watchful eye on him. The village had not been told yet that an imposter posing to be Porugl came and took Maie away. This would unsettle the village and cause hysteria amongst the villagers.

"There are some evil forces at work here, my chief," said Damba.

"Damba, you and the boys go with a war party and check on Porugl and his wife," said Anga Kumugl, "Sleep and rest boys, you will leave tomorrow early in the morning."

The next day, Damba and the boys left Bogl. Kimbi had gone earlier after overhearing the conversation between Damba and Anga. Kimbi came to the entrance of Bogl, but Porugl and Waine had left already.

"They didn't tell us where they were going. The two left in a hurry," said the warriors.

Kimbi didn't hear the rest of it and left. He saw the fresh footprints. When the guards told Damba and the boys Kimbi had gone after Porugl, they pursued. They walked across the Kakam range when they heard noises coming across the river. A dark patch of people moved into Dawake, the Kumoku village.

"This must be all the tribes across the river," said Mange.

"We have to warn our people, return quickly to Chief Anga and inform him what is happening," said Damba to one of the warriors.

Just then, a commotion started on this side of the river. Voices began rising out of the Daneku village. They had no allegiance with Tambaiku or Kumoku and were the most likely to be hit first. They called out to the other tribes that they noticed the large gathering across the river. They appealed for calm and proposed themselves as peace mediators. Damba and the troupe stood listening. No reply came from the Kumoku. Then, across the Kakam range, the Endaku and Kumanku started shouting. People shouted everywhere.

"Look up there," said one warrior, pointing to the top of the Kakam range.

A large crowd of warriors gathered at the top.

"These are the Kombuglku, the last tribe in Kondaland. Word must have got to them already. Things are moving fast. We need to get to Porugl and Maie before it gets out of hand."

"They are coming down," said the same warrior.

"We have to move," said Damba.

Porugl and Waine passed the Kakam ridge into the Mokma Mountains and stood gazing down. The wind blew against them and they saw Gandia with Bindekai in the background.

To his other side lay the lands before the Porugl

Mountains. Below them, the dreaded Sikewake lay hidden under the morning clouds. If he understood correctly, the imposter and Maie would be here. If Kerwanba wanted revenge, she would do it here. Porugl and Waine made their way down the edge of the Mokma Mountain to Sikewake.

"Are you sure this is the place?" said Waine.

"I hope so," said Porugl.

The people were moving frantically about in all the villages. Women tugged on their animals with large bilum bags on their heads and children on their backs. They had to seek refuge elsewhere, away from the threat of war, while their husbands prepared to defend their land. Pigs squealed, children cried and men berated their wives for taking time exiting the area.

Porugl and Waine paused, hearing the commotion and dread how it would turn out. Porugl knew he had to end Kerwanba once and for all to protect Kondaland from devolving into Kundawii. Kerwanba would then rule both the Underworld and Outerworld; an outcome much more frightening.

"Porugl," yelled Maie.

The two broke off from their thoughts and peered down. Below them, they could see Maie, standing near the cliff's edge, the place where Porugl had jumped. She gazed across. Kerwanba coiled around another figure and then swerved around her.

"There she is," said Waine.

"Maie," called Porugl, but his voice got lost along the

way with the wind. "I have to get closer," he said and trod down the treacherous rock face. "Waine, we have to get to that protruding rock."

Waine wanted to go around the cliff and come behind Kerwanba. But saw the look on Porugl's face.

"Do you love Porugl?" said the snake.

Maie held her breath as the gigantic serpent moved towards her. The scales of her body shone and reflected the colors of the rainbow in the morning sunlight.

"Do you love Porugl?" she hissed again.

"Yeeesss," she screamed.

Porugl heard her scream and grappled at the rock formation to move faster to the protruding rock. Kerwanba squeezed a little harder around the imposter and turned him around to show Maie.

"Are you willing to give your life for him?" said Kerwanba. "Either you die, or he dies. You choose. Your husband was very brave to save the village, to come back to you. Will you be brave for him? Will you sacrifice your life to save him, like he did for you?"

"I will," said Maie.

"Your husband jumped over the Sikewake cliff. I promise, if you jump over, I will let your husband live, and she squeezed tighter on the imposter.

"Ahhh," cried the imposter.

All the while, the minions were working in her mind. They whispered all sorts of things and said she married Porugl to sacrifice herself for him. It could have been Dengg, but Dengg would never lay down her life for Porugl in order to save the Akenku tribe. The great snake moved closer, forcing Maie to walk closer to the edge of the Sikewake cliff.

"Maie, so many people have died, and many more will die. You can stop it. Just jump over the cliff and die for your husband," continued the minions. "Your death can set everyone free."

Maie stood at the cliff's edge. She recalled the time when she saw Kondai, distraught and ready to take her own life.

"You have to be strong for Porugl like I was strong for him," came Kondai's words into her mind. "I'm sorry, my child, that you will not see daylight and I will have taken your life. You and I, we have to save your father," she said, stroking her stomach.

Each word came out with pain and her sobbing increased. Her shoulders shook uncontrollably as the tears gushed out, moving closer and closer to the edge. If being strong meant the ultimate sacrifice to save Porugl's life, she would do it. Her only sorrow lay in her womb. She looked across to the Mokma Mountains, opened her hands, and closed her eyes. In that moment, she saw in her mind's eye a terrific flash of lightning across the land. The thunder that followed ruptured the skies and rain fell in torrents. She saw a man standing in the rain. He had a tough face, defined by time and experiences. The intermittent lightning showed his piercing eyes, which Maie could not avoid. In his hand, he held the *kuglang* or scepter of leadership, and he glared at her with a gaze that entered her eyes right into her mind. Behind him, a multitude of warriors, as far as the eye could see, stood ready, and the rain poured.

"Maie don't," shouted Porugl. "I am here."

Maie and the serpent both peered up and saw Porugl standing with Waine close behind. Quite a distance still remained in between.

"Porugl," she cried and looked at the imposter. "What's happening?"

"That's not me," he said.

Just then, Kerwanba tossed Kewand Kumugl's shrunken body out. The body fell to the ground, broken and twisted. Kerwanba had no more need for him. Porugl felt sorry for the man who had been like a father to him in the Underworld. He knew Kerwanba must have given him no choice.

"Well, this is good a reunion at the place where it all began," said Kerwanba, rising up.

"She has nothing to do with this. Let her—"

"She has everything to do with this," shrieked Kerwanba. "What, she has not told you? She is with child. I will never let your lineage carry on from here."

At hearing this, Porugl ground his teeth and took out three of his arrows. Waine did the same. He shook his head, with his eyes fixated on Kerwanba, and placed three arrows onto his bow. He didn't choose this life; he got caught up in it. His own tribe threw him down a pit because of something he didn't fully understand. His desire to go back home kept him sane all this time in the Underworld, culminating in his escape from the jaws of death in this very place. And now, this same monster kept taunting him, telling him that he had to die in order to save the only thing he truly loved. The news of Maie being pregnant caught him by surprise. The legacy of Kande Kumugl must never end.

"Are you man enough?" called Kerwanba up to Porugl. "I have broken the balance and I alone will restore it, but you never knew that, did you? You only knew what you were told."

"I know enough that they sent you to the Underworld, because in the beginning you were a witch."

"Your genealogy will end here. There will be nothing to remind this world of you. I will make sure of it once I break every bone in your body," she said and coiled herself around Maie.

"Don't let her get into your head," said Waine.

"Put her down. This is between you and me," said Porugl.

"If you want her, come and get her," said the serpent and hoisted her up and down. "Your father, the weakling, begged for mercy just before they chopped off his head, he—"

"Come and get me," shouted Porugl and leapt into the air, plunging down with his bow and arrows aimed at Kerwanba.

"No," shouted Waine.

The ancient serpent sprung up and opened her ugly jaws. She had unhinged her mandible to gobble the incoming Porugl completely. The wide opening of her mouth made targeting her throat and forked tongue easier. The venom fangs shone. He saw where he could land and avoid her razor-sharp teeth. Further down her body, she tightened the grip around Maie.

Porugl released three arrows into the serpent's mouth while in midair. The arrows struck the serpent's gullet and the inner parts of her upper and lower jaw. The serpent felt a stinging sensation as the wide tipped arrows, crafted to cause maximum damage, struck her in different places. It stung her, and she released her grip on Maie just as Porugl came crashing into Kerwanba's jaws with his quiver of arrows still on his back. Kerwanba felt Porugl and snapped her jaws shut, but to her surprise, her mouth couldn't close. Porugl's bow lodged itself firmly into the lower and upper part of her jaws, and he held onto it with all his might. She squeezed harder and felt the tips of the bow dig into her flesh. The forked tongue found its way around Porugl's body and coiled itself around his neck. He ran out of breath and the snake's gullet opened. Her muscles began to move Porugl in. He had to do something about the forked tongue or he would pass out at any moment and be ingested.

The serpent shook her head vigorously, but the bow didn't move at all. She tried to crush the bow by applying more force, only to feel the bow dig deeper into her flesh. Black blood seeped out from where the edge of the bow had sunk in. She shook and battered her head against the rocks. Still, the bow remained. She then opened her mouth extremely wide to free the bow, but nothing happened. The serpent didn't understand what object stopped her from closing her jaws, nor did she have any clue how to deal with this. All the while, she continued to ingest Porugl deeper down her gullet. The forked tongue kept its tight grip around his neck and just before it snapped his neck, Porugl cut it off with his axe. Kerwanba felt the loss of feeling to her tongue and crunched her jaws harder, sending one end of the bow protruding out between her eyes.

Waine already made his way down and secured Maie when they saw the forked tongue fall out of Kerwanba's jaws, writhing and twisting itself on the ground. This snake vomited all the dead animals of the Underworld she had ingested out in a gush. The stench was horrible. Porugl suffocated in the blob of vomit that covered him and felt the snake's digestive juices working on his body. The serpent's sharp teeth cut him as he hung in the snake's mouth

"We have to get him out," shrieked Maie.

"I know, but how?" said Waine.

The serpent spasmed uncontrollably, flinging herself everywhere in an attempt to dislodge the bow and to disturb Porugl so he could remove his grasp of the bow. Waine and Maie made a run for cover out of the swiveling snake's way. Waine shot one arrow, and it landed squarely in one of Kerwanba's eyes. The snake felt the painful itch in her eye and shook herself with significant force. She sprung up again into the air. Waine and Maie gave way as she landed with a tremendous thud. Waine kept sending arrows into her body and eyes until his quiver was empty. She lost her balance and rolled over the edge of the cliff. Porugl nearly got swallowed with all the vomit, making the bow slippery. The serpent lost all focus, but its body movements increased in intensity as it bumped and smashed itself against the rock walls of the Sikewake cliff.

"We have to help her," cried Gurr-toki.

"She is on her own now," said Agandua. "If she comes out alive from this, you and I, will join Kimin-ege."

"I will go and do what I can," said Gurr-toki.

Maie and Waine heard the rubble and loose rocks dislodged as the serpent crashed below.

Thoughts of her legacy and ending came rushing into her as she bumped against the sharp edges of the cliff. The pain didn't matter; the ending did. She couldn't return to the Underworld with the bow still wedged in her jaws. She would be a laughingstock. If she had to die killing Porugl, then it would happen that way, she thought. She clenched her jaws further, ignoring the pain. The two ends of the bow stuck out of her head. One end came out between her eyes and the other below her lower jaw. Even the bow string showed no signs of giving in and separated her flesh from where it came into contact.

Suddenly, with a mighty screech that reverberated all throughout the land, Kerwanba launched herself into the air. She landed with a sickening thump on a sharp piece of rock at the foot of the cliff. The bump knocked Porugl out and he let go his grip on the bow.

A loud explosion burst through the different realms in the Underworld. All creatures and beings felt excited and scared at the same time. Kerwanba had broken the balance and engaged directly with the Outerworld. She had opened the door. All the creatures of the different realms flooded out of Ugl Komboglo. Nondo and Milime stood close to Goglko. Some curious beings had already gone down to the cliff. They wanted to be the first to stand over her dead body and rejoice.

"Kerwanba's still moving," said Maie. "What's happening with Porugl?"

Something blotted out the sun, and both looked up.

"What's that?" said Maie.

"Looks like a rain cloud," said Waine.

"It's moving fast."

"It's no rain cloud, birds, it's an enormous flock of birds."

The tumult of bird screeches mixed with human voices filled the sky as the flock made its way closer. The Mokanku, Bonoku, Dembeku, Koleku, Mingeku and Kawaiku who had joined forces with the Tambaiku and Kumoku assembled at the banks of the river, ready to cross over, when they saw the birds' flight. Across the river, the remaining Akenku, with the Wakiku, Daneku, Endaku, Kumanku and Kombuglku prepared to defend their lands, also saw the menacing sight. The large flock of birds dived and circled around Kerwanba and then returned higher up. Some of the birds moved in an unnatural way. As they swooped down, the tribes got a better look at them. Some had the heads of snakes, lizards, and worms. Others had the faces of dogs and wild boars, while others had human faces. It was a ghastly sight.

"Kumo kwimbos, responding to their queen," said Damba to the warriors.

"Where is Porugl?" asked Anga, who had just arrived.

"Inside the great snake, she gulped him. We don't know if he is still alive," said Waine.

Chief Anga welcomed the large troupe of Kombuglku warriors, who joined them. He told the Kombuglku they would be the last to defend their lands if the conflict advanced further.

The earth spun around Kerwanba and she remained motionless. She had arrows all over her body and in her mouth, her tongue cut out and vertebrae cracked. She remained still, hoping that the fall had killed him. Then she felt him move. He grappled for the bow. Kerwanba locked her jaws and continued to swallow him. She mustered all her strength and crawled out to the river.

"She is trying to drown him," said Anga. I want our marksmen to shelter the banks with arrows. Do not let her reach the river. "I need warriors to go and hack that beast to death."

The circling birds saw the hail of arrows towards Kerwanba. While some kept swirling around, others targeted the warriors and came in hard on them.

"Take them down," shouted Damba.

16

The Beginning of Kundawii

Birds were falling out of the sky like rain, but some got through and grabbed the warriors, lifting them up into the air and flinging them into the cliff. The warriors all around heard their screams as they crashed against the rocks.

"Don't be still. Fire your arrows and keep moving around," ordered Anga.

Arrows blocked Kerwanba's path to the river. Some had already lodged in her. Paralysis would set in at any time. The birds changed their focus and came down for her. The whole multitude swooped in on her and lifted her out. Warriors who were sent to hack her to death watched as the enormous snake became airborne. They fired their arrows, but the birds attacked them.

The Wakiku called out to the other tribes to concentrate all their firepower on the unearthly sight. Kerwanba's weight with Porugl still inside slowed the bird's efforts. They rose out of *Sekiwake* steadily. Warriors went to strategic locations on hilltops, ridges and peaks.

The birds covered Kerwanba's body totally, and the arrows shot by the warriors missed as the birds rose higher and higher.

"Where will they take the serpent?" asked one warrior.

"No idea," replied another.

"If she lives, we are all doomed," said Anga. "We will devolve into Kundawii."

"Are we doomed, my chief?" said a young warrior.

"If we know where they are taking her, we can attack there."

The warriors shuddered. The little they heard about the Kundawii had sent shivers through them. The blob in the sky got smaller.

"They will take her to a distant place to heal," said Damba. "I think they will go up north."

"You four, return to Bindekai and see where they are taking her," said Anga to his warriors.

As Damba had predicted, the blob in the sky slowly made its way north, following the river. Suddenly, the screech of a Kekemba sent the birds into different directions. Two great eagles came down from the Bindekai peaks. The remaining birds struggled to keep the heavy snake in mid-air. The scampering birds came back and restored the height while others attacked the two eagles. The reduced number of birds couldn't handle the weight and they flew quite low. Higher up, the eagles fought against the birds. The snake approached Gandia and the enemy warriors saw the strange sight. The two eagles couldn't handle the multitude of birds and returned to Bindekai.

Suddenly, the air around Kondaland shattered with a caw that reverberated all the way into Koraland. Everyone gazed into the atmosphere and the birds scattered everywhere. They had heard the screech of an eagle before, but this one came from the giant of all eagles.

A mighty Kekemba stretched its wings on Bindekai. It had just returned from a hunting trip and saw its parents driven back by evil, possessed birds. In one swoop, the great eagle leapt into the air and came down like a huge arrow towards the snake. Other birds saw its sheer size and hid where they had taken refuge. The possessed birds returned to their normal figures of humans, men, and women. They came out pretending that nothing had happened and joined the crowd of people who had gathered.

This great eagle would take over authority of the skies over Kondaland and even Koraland. It had clean shiny feathers, a hooked and hard beak, and a powerful gaze. It came straight for the snake. The birds carrying Kerwanba saw this awesome yet frightening sight and dropped the snake and fled. It landed with half its body in the river and the other half on the banks.

The Kekemba did a low flyby over the warriors gathered with the Kumoku. They cowered, expecting to be thrashed by the eagles' massive talons. Then he went across the river and did the same to the tribes gathered there. They rejoiced and praised the Kekemba. The Akenku wept tears of joy. Everyone knew they shared a special bond with Kekemba. The magnificent bird flew back to the peaks of Bindekai to the topmost rock, a spot where all great eagles before it stood and established their supremacy and gazed down.

"To the river," shouted the Akenku warriors.

Maie and Waine hurried after the tribes as they charged to the snake. A hail of arrows greeted them as they arrived on the opposite bank. Maie and Waine watched from a distance as warriors on either side exchanged arrows. A war party from Tambaiku and Kumoku advanced down in a long line of shields.

"Defenders move in," shouted Anga.

Wakiku and Daneku lifted their shields and advanced across the river. The opposing side met them in the river and they engaged. Slashed bodies swept down with the current, making the river red.

"Move, move," shouted Anga, as other warriors started jumping into the river.

More and more warriors piled into the river and towards the ancient serpent. The battle raged around Kerwanba, making it quite difficult to get close.

The snake opened its mouth, taking in an enormous volume of water. The cold water shook Porugl out of his daze. He coughed and struggled to breathe. The snake's throat muscles tightened around him. He moved his arms around. He could feel his axe. With a little more motion, he would get hold of it. The snake opened its mouth and another gush of water came in. He coughed again and again. Kerwanba's senses became unsteady. She had to drown him. The intake of water allowed Porugl to move his arm, and he grappled for his axe.

It began to rain and several thunder claps shook everyone. The sky rumbled as if disagreeing with the happenings below. The river changed its color to brown. Porugl heard the increased tapping of raindrops and intensified his reach for the axe. A loud din approached the warriors, and they scurried back.

The heavy rains had caused the river flow to increase quickly and rise, which caught some warriors off guard. People watching on either side scampered to find shelter. Others wanted to know how it would end and stood in the rain near the banks, watching as the flow lifted the snake. A boulder stopped the snake from being carried away.

Maie stood close to Waine, never taking her eyes off the snake. She thought she saw the serpent move. Then she saw it. Kerwanba used her tail to push herself into the fast-flowing river.

"Waine," she said. "Kerwanba is moving. She is moving towards the current."

Waine squinted his eyes to see. The rain eased, but the current still maintained its strength, stopping anyone from crossing. It would be suicide to cross, knowing that anyone taken down would be smashed into the Sikewake rock face. An arrow swooshed past them, hitting the trunk of a tree.

"Get down," said Waine, and they both crouched.

Soon a volley of swooshing sounds came through the trees and the leaves. A war party made its way to the snake.

"Marksmen, get into position," said Anga. "Fire."

Mange. Ningir and Bauglo could not hold themselves and rushed to the bank. They stopped opposite the snake and sent arrows over to the war party.

Something pounded the snake's stomach from the inside. The snake felt it and increased the wriggling of her tail. She had much less muscular control with all the arrows and injuries to her body. She moved to the fast current while pounding kept on. Then an axe finally broke through. They saw a hand reaching out and cutting away at the tear in the serpent's skin. Kewand Kumugl had given him this special axe just before he left the Underworld. It had a powerful spell to sever anything in its path. After a couple of blows to the skin and flesh, Porugl fell out of the snake.

Loud shrieking and screaming followed as Porugl fell into the river. The Akenku and the other tribes rejoiced while the Tambaiku and Kumoku increased their arrows across the river and towards Porugl. He bent down into the water, using the snake's body as cover. He bobbed his head up quickly and went down again and heard a hail of arrows pass by. The enemy watched all corners of the snake's body. He could dive, but where would he go? Across the river, Mange, Bauglo and Ningir, quickly made a rope from dried *komba* or red pandanus leaves. They shouted to him and indicated that they would be throwing the rope across.

"It's those pests again. Shoot them. Why are you shooters missing?" shouted Bindi Kumugl.

Arrows kept preventing the young warriors from hurling the rope over. They hid behind the big marshes but were undecided how they would get the rope across. Porugl had to get his bow out of the snake's head. Everyone on both sides watched in amazement as he went back into the hole he just cut, wriggled up the snake's gullet and yanked one end of the bow down. He then pulled the free end towards him, releasing the bow, and came out again.

"That must be a special bow," said Anga.

Arrows on both sides reduced in number. The war party moved closer to the snake. They didn't know how to approach. Porugl had no way to move as the tide maintained its strength. The snake's eyes twitched and irregular muscle spasms rocked her body.

The boys threw the rope across and he grabbed it and threw his bow over. It flew over their heads. Porugl didn't like taking chances with his bow. Just as he flung himself into the river, someone came out of nowhere and jumped onto him. Both went into the fast current. The advancing party forgot their fear of the serpent and watched as the two heads got swallowed up in the current. Porugl kept his other hand on the rope and the other hand on his axe. The river tossed and turned both men. His assailant clung to his back and attempted to cut him with his axe, but the river's current disturbed his aim. Porugl swung his axe backward, but the current disturbed him also. The boys and everyone on both sides saw them being swept away and gulped by the dips in the river.

The rope tightened, and the boys heaved with all their might. They made little progress being strained under the weight of two men and the current. Everyone moved down along the banks of the river. For that moment, they forgot their purpose there. The rope snapped and the three boys rushed down.

Porugl felt no tension in the rope and let it go. He had crossed strong currents before and knew they would be sheltered from the boulders and rocks in the river because of the height the river had reached. The assailant enclosed his arms around his neck and, with his other hand, swung his axe inward towards Porugl's body and face. The river's fast current canceled his efforts. They dipped into the river and then came up again. Porugl's other hand tried to release the assailant's grip while his other hand held onto his axe. He saw the strength of the river working against the slashing and waited for the right moment. The Sikewake rock face loomed ahead and coming up quickly.

The next dip pulled both men right down with all their weight. His feet felt a boulder, and he pushed against it with all his might and spun over. The force of the water assisted his motion and flung the assailant forward. The assailant struggled to swim to the bank. Both men saw a tree fallen across the river. The assailant grabbed a branch and lifted himself onto the trunk. He stood with his axe and waited. Porugl came in the same way and also grabbed a branch. The man walked steadily on the slippery trunk towards Porugl and swung his axe as he put his hand on the trunk. Porugl moved his hand away and clung to the trunk with his other hand. The assailant swung again but fell into the river as two arrows pierced his body. The boys rushed to Porugl and pulled him up.

They sat on the banks for a while for Porugl to get his breath back. The warriors on the other side saw him being saved and didn't continue. It was over.

"Who was that man?" he asked.

"I got a good look at him while he stood on the tree trunk. It was Kimbi, Dingan's uncle," said Bauglo.

"Kerwanba?"

"The great Kekemba came and took the ancient serpent away. Kerwanba is dead," said Ningir.

The words hit him like nothing before, and he cried. He let out a sorrowful wail. The thoughts of all the people who died, the houses, gardens and families destroyed and lives lost came flooding into his mind. He thought of his father, his son from Dikamb and his unborn child with Maie and, despite the rain still falling down, his tears were hot and kept coming.

Kerwanba ended and signaled the beginning of the great tumult. She broke the balance no one else could restore. Her death would not stop the events already in motion. The rain began to pick up again as black clouds covered the whole of Kondaland and smudged the sunlight. Winds blew and blew with ferocity, forcing trees to bend over. Leaves and branches got blown away.

Tribes on both sides of the river's retreated hastily, no longer interested in winning the battle. The early villagers made it into their homes before a torrent of hailstones poured out from the sky. Those who had no cover saw the hailstones, roughly the size of a clenched fist, and sprinted to the nearest house or cave. Others did not make it. People in the house heard loud noises on their roofs. It didn't take long for the hailstones to break through the thatched roofs. Families ran out of their houses only to be pummeled to death. The known caves filled quickly. Humans stood side by side with creatures, beings and spirits from all the realms in the Underworld. They would ask questions later and gazed out to see the large chucks of ice destroying every tree, food crop and animal. Rocks and boulders on either side of the river's banks got dislodged as the river volume and current increased. Loud crashes could be heard as chunks of ground on slopes tumbled down. They heard the wails of woman and children amidst the din caused by the elements but could not do anything. The hailstorm did not discriminate and destroyed everything in Kondaland.

Others, who were lucky to escape the hail, came into the known caves all drenched, while some brought with them injured family members. No house withstood the force of the hail and no domesticated animal survived. The large hail stones came down with force and smashed everything in its path.

Creatures scampered to return to their realms but couldn't enter the Underworld. They tried different openings and routes without success. Many of the creatures and beings came to Goglko to get an explanation. He just stood there, shaking his head. Men, women, children, creatures, beings and animals from both worlds took refuge together in rock shelters and caves.

"Betrayer," shouted one of the creatures and pointed to Gurr-toki and Agandua.

Gurr-toki had been trying to remain inconspicuous when one of the creatures recognised her. Every being gazed at her. Those who stood beside backed away.

"I told her not to help Kerwanba, but she went and brought the birds," said Agandua, trying to distance himself from her.

"You shut your mouth," said another being.

They closed in on the two minions.

The balance of life was broken, and there was only one outcome. Her death signaled the start of the Kundawii.

Glossary

Agandua-minion to Kerwanba

Aglang-the wail a Simbu woman does in appreciation

Akenku-Porugl's tribe

Ambai kango-courting between men and women

Amugl birr-ceremony to share pandanus

Bindi Kumugl- Chief of Tambaiku

Bindekai-sharp peak at the edge of Gandia village

Bogl-Wakiku village

Dawake-Kumoku village

Dee Kumugl-Kumoku chief

Dikamb-Porugl's (gigl ambu), wife in the underworld

Dingan-Kande Kumugl's illegitimate son and Gamba's half brother

Druwagle-Damba's wife

Gamba-Porugl's father

Gandia Murr-endless pit of Gandia

Gandia-Porugl's village where the Akenku tribe lives

Gigl ambu-female spirit being

Gigl-general term for spirit being

Gigl yagl-male spirit being

Goglko-one of the creatures in the Underworld with special powers

Goimbu-Bindi Kumugl's war commander

Gotndagl-Porugl's ancestor, Kande Kumugl's grandfather

Gurr toki-minion to Kerwanba

Gwika tree-a special tree with healing powers in its leaf growing in the underworld. Air seeps out of its leaf.

Halfling-offspring off a gigl ambu and a human

Irawam Togklumba-one eyed monster

Ka kango-special speech only delivered by chiefs

~~~

Kakep-the middle man or woman who goes between the bride and groom's family organising the marriage

Kama Kumugl-third human to be thrown into the pit

Kamawagle-name of river running beside Porugl's house in Gandia

Kande Kumugl-Gamba's father and Porugl's grandfather and chief of Akenku

Kekemba-mythical eagle

Kerwanba- ancient snake of the Underworld

Kewand Kumugl-first human to be thrown into the pit

Kimin ege-minion to Kerwanba

Kogun Kumugl-chief of Kumoku

Komba-red pandanus

Komba bir-a ceremony to share Komba

Kondaland-the whole are where the tribes speak one language

Koraland-the lands to the south of Kondaland

Kondai-Gamba's wife and Porugl's mother

Kuglang-the sceptre of leadership

Kumo kwimbo-a human possessing an evil spirit

Kumoku-enemy tribe to the Akenku

Kumugl-title of a leader which is said after the leader's name

Kwi Kumugl-second human to be thrown into the pit

Makan nem-another being of the underworld known commonly as the landlord

Mana-mother

Mando-Chief of dwarf realm

Mangra-the word that invites the crowd to shout, usually in approval of something like a speech

Milime-a gigl ambu who married the dwarf called Nondo

Mondaugl-Tambaiku village

Nina-father

Ningir-Sie's son and Porugl's cousin

Noglkipokrande-magic word to open the underworld to outsiders

Nondo-dwarf who healed Porugl

Okun Kumugl- Kande Kumugl's father

Outerworld-reference to the lands above the Underworld where humans live

Ormar-Custodian of Akenku in the absence of a chief

Porugl-the main character

Sie-Gamba's brother

Sikewake–the place where three rivers come crashing into each other

Ugl Kombuglo-the cave entrance near Sikewake where Porugl came out from the Underworld

Underling-general term for all creatures and beings living in the Underworld

Underworld-the realms beneath the earth where mythical creatures and beings live

Wandike-the act of taking refuge in another village

Yal Wai-the local Shaman, medicine man and trusted advisor to Kande Kumugl

Yal yungu-house where only the men live (men's house)

Yer arrai-deadly assault arrow

The Author wishes to acknowledge and thank Francisca Kuri, my wife, for making suggestions and editing.

The Author also wishes to thank First Nations Writers Festival ("FNWF") for creating the avenue for writers of the Greater Pacific to expose their talents. The FNWF has filled a void that writers in the Greater Pacific have struggled with; and that is a platform to showcase the ways, cultures, history, traditions and interests of the people in the Greater Pacific.

The Author acknowledges the efforts of FNWF to publish Porugl - The Atrocity of Kerwanba.

Thank you FNWF.

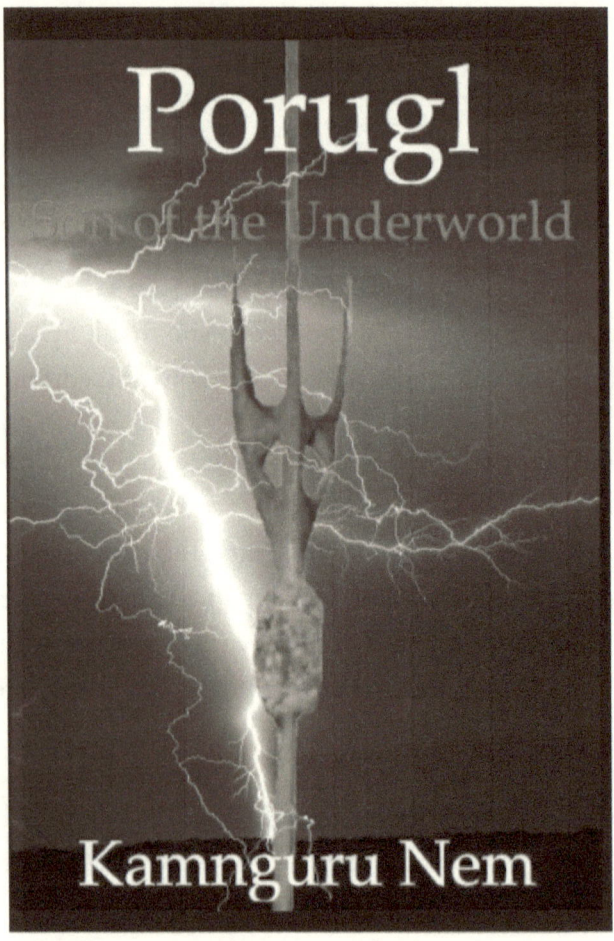

Porugl
Son of the Underworld

Kamnguru Nem

Life in Gandia takes a turn for the worst when an innocent male child is thrown down an endless pit.

Secrets that lay hidden for ages are about to be revealed and what many thought to be myth is about to become real

Family and tribal legacy that ruled all life in Gandia is on the verge of collapsing and the only man who can restore it, has to come out of the earth fighting. But the only thing standing in his way is the ancient serpent called Kerwanba.